Siren's Call

DCI Garrick - book 8

M.G. Cole

TANGLEBOX BOOKS

SIREN'S CALL
A DCI Garrick mystery - Book 8

Copyright © 2024 by Max Cole (M.G.Cole)

All rights reserved. No part of this publication may be reproduced, distributed, or transmitted in any form or by any means, including photocopying, recording, or other electronic or mechanical methods, without the prior written permission of the publisher, except in the case of brief quotations embodied in critical reviews and certain other non-commercial uses permitted by copyright law.

Cover art: Shutterstock

SIREN'S CALL

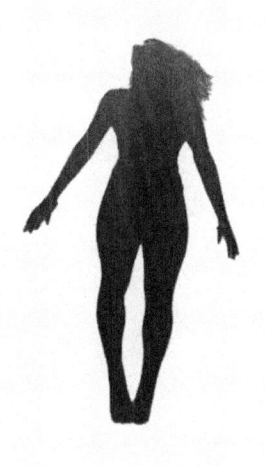

Chapter One

They say drowning is just like falling asleep. A softness that tugs at the chest and gently lowers the dark veil across perception, easing pains and soothing despair until there is nothing but darkness and the soft pulse of the watery embrace, as if one were returning to the womb, returning to the very moment of life.

They are wrong.

Drowning is an act of violation. An intense moment of battle to prevent life being crushed from the body. And even at the last breath, the brain is still active. Still watching. Still silently screaming in the face of the inevitable. Unable to do anything other than die.

The woman clung to the rope bound so close to the gunwale that it painfully dug into the folds of skin in her palms every time they crested a white-capped wave, which they were doing with increased rhythm as the pilot pushed the throttle stops harder. She swore that each wave was growing bigger as they briefly took to the air, only to bellyflop hard on the other side. She had been feeling nauseous since they departed. Only the frigid air blasted across her face had helped quell the feeling. Then the driving rain had soaked her to the skin, further chilling her to the bone.

Her mind was reeling, unable to fully process what was happening, and what she had just witnessed.

Another jolt sent ripples of pain down her back and through her chest. She tried to crouch low to counteract the storm and movement, but steely fingers gripped her upper arm and pulled her upright.

"No, you don't," the man growled so close to her ear that she could smell his tobacco-heavy breath despite the wind.

She had fought with them before, and now they were adamant about making the rest of the journey a living hell for her. The jerking movement of the boat was now causing her head to spin. The strength was ebbing from her body. She blinked rapidly, trying to stay awake. It was essential that she was alert enough to make her break for freedom the moment any opportunity arose. If she were to stay their prisoner, then her life was going to be measured only in hours.

With blurring vision, she suddenly lashed out. Her elbow blindly slugged the man behind her. A half-recalled self-defence class raised her foot in a half-hearted kick. Her boot connected with some force, and she heard a smashing noise as another assailant crashed into the cabin. A burning smell from behind caught her attention, and the pitch of the outboard motor changed.

Then the illusion of freedom was snatched from her as something heavy connected with the back of her head and the world turned black.

And, as weakness overwhelmed her, and she felt herself

Siren's Call

topple sideways, her last thoughts questioned if she even had minutes left. An iconic fate for one who had cheated death twice.

Her captors had ensured there would be no third time.

Chapter Two

David Garrick was coming to realise that a *normal* life was something to be coveted, rather than one he'd previously regarded as dull and tedious. He'd spent the last two months off work, marvellously, on full pay, recuperating with a range of physical therapy and long sessions with a therapist. It was a similar pattern to what he'd gone through before, except this time he looked forward to both sessions. It was the highlight of his week to unload his inner angst and demons, then escape back to his humdrum home to spend time in front of the television with Wendy, whose womb was becoming larger with each passing moment. Their daughter was due in four weeks, but Garrick suspected if she took after him, she would undoubtedly be late. Life was ridiculously *normal*.

The trauma of his past life had miraculously become a blank slate for him. Not from amnesia or the countless knocks on the head he'd received, but from professional hand-holding that had taught him not to dwell on things that could not be fixed. And his past was certainly an ocean of the unfixable.

He'd learned the art of thinking about himself and in doing so had found a fresh flush of new life. He'd joined his local David Lloyd gym and after several rounds on the various torture devices, he'd settled on a running machine as his weapon of choice. He'd even taken to listening to podcasts as he pounded away, barely beyond walking pace, with the distant dream of achieving a 5 km non-stop run. So far, he'd just peaked at 2 km, but the overwhelming wave of satisfaction and endorphins was keeping him going. He'd even lost weight, although Wendy was too preoccupied to notice, and almost everybody else he saw was operating in a professional capacity, so they tended not to comment on his physical appearance.

To top things off, he'd also downloaded a mindfulness app and a Dummies Guide to Yoga. That had become his greatest secret shame - he didn't even want to tell Wendy. But he was loving the simple pleasures found in yoga.

As his return date back to work loomed, and the pregnancy shuffled inevitably forward, they spent an intense week shopping for baby clothes, toys, and furniture. While he had enjoyed strolling around Ikea, when it came to putting the furniture up, he needed every self-help coping tool in his arsenal not to throw the bloody thing out of the window.

But Garrick was a social creature at heart. That's one reason he had been drawn to police work. By the time his hiatus was over, he was genuinely looking forward to human contact with his team, which he'd been denied other than the occasional WhatsApp message. The last few days before The Return saw his anxiety levels rise as he wondered what had changed and what had been overlooked. The worry of having to repair problems in his absence was beginning to erase the tranquil benefits he had earned over the last couple of months.

Of course, he needn't have been too concerned when he entered Maidstone Police Station. It was as if he'd entered a time capsule and was merely greeted with a wave of head bobs, a few muttered grunts, and the most minimalist of greetings from his old friend, Detective Constable Lord, and Detective Sergeant Chibarameze Okon, who was so efficient she threatened to upstage him.

The only noticeable difference was the frostiness between DC Fanta Liu and DC Sean Wilkes, who were in a relationship together, although Garrick avoided pressing the issue like the plague. It was only when they brought the atmosphere in the office down a peg or two that he regretted not addressing the situation earlier.

The team's current workload tracking down an organised gang stealing luxury cars en route to the border across Kent and Sussex, had turned their affectionately named 'murder board' into something that belonged on *Top Gear*. It was covered with images of supercars they could only dream about owning, instead of the usual mug shots and pictures of corpses. He had to admit that it brightened the place up.

And with that, Garrick found he had abruptly drifted into phase two of normality. Some dull, but safe detective work while sharing the occasional swift phone call with Wendy throughout the day. Very little progress had been made on the case, but at least nobody was dying.

Once again, he began to find the stress of the world was dissolving around him. He was finally getting the hang of a regular life and, for the first time in a long time, the team had a social event looming on the horizon. DS Okon's wedding.

Chib had been forced to delay her wedding due to work events once, and then a second time because her partner had fallen ill. But now, their wedding was happening - and this was to be no small occasion. Okon's entire Nigerian heritage was on display, and to Garrick's eyes, it felt as if a carnival had come to town.

The team generally respected each other's personal lives, although Garrick's own circumstances had been central to various cases recently, so it felt as if everybody knew everything there was to know about him. But when asked to elaborate on his team's family lives, he struggled. Other than Fanta and Sean's annoying relationship, he knew Harry was married, but couldn't swear if he had kids. And they had known one another since they were regular coppers walking the beat. Perhaps that's why, when he met Okon's betrothed for the first time, he was more than a little surprised. The fact that Gwen was white hadn't surprised him; Chib was one of the most open-minded people he knew. That his Detective Sergeant was gay was a surprise. Some detective he was. He silently berated himself for even thinking there should be any signs, whichever way she decided to sail.

Chib's family was religious, very loud with it. Garrick felt it was a corner of religion he couldn't get on board with, a feeling he conveyed to every other religion he'd encountered. They were also very accepting. They had embraced Gwen, a soft-spoken Irish girl from Dublin, without hesitation.

The service in the Registry Office had been so packed that Garrick and the other members of the team could barely hear from where they were crushed into a rear corner. The evening do put Garrick in mind of scenes from *Apocalypse*

Now. The massive hall was the venue for a carnival of drunken partying where everybody was forced to dance to a wall of music that gradually numbed the ears.

Wendy had declined the invitation, which at first had annoyed him, but he'd come to realise, as he was increasingly wont to do, that it was yet another of her excellent judgement calls. He should listen to her a little bit more. Maybe then things wouldn't turn out so bad.

He couldn't shirk the feeling that Chib was slightly embarrassed by it all. So, after three too-many beers, he had gathered the CID team around her and forced them all to dance to a pulsing rhythm that rightfully would have deserved its own choreographed routine. Despite his initial reluctance to attend, it was turning into one of the best nights Garrick had had in years, even when Chib and Gwen insisted the team don something more traditional.

David Garrick tugged at the collar of his traditional Nigerian agbada, a resplendent robe of deep blue with intricate golden embroidery. Although he was dressed more in line with the guests around him, he still felt like a fish out of water. But he had to admit, the garment had a certain regal flair. Beside him, Chib, resplendent in her own vibrant green and gold dress, grinned broadly at his discomfort.

"Relax, Guv. It's a celebration, not an interrogation."

"Easy for you to say," Garrick muttered. "You grew up with this. I feel like I'm at a fancy-dress party gone wrong."

Chib laughed, a melodious sound that carried over the pulsing beat of the music. "Just wait until the dancing starts. You'll fit right in."

With that, the wedding reception stepped into full swing with a kaleidoscope of colour and sound. The bride and bride sat at the head table, their faces aglow with joy. Around them, hundreds of guests, a sea of brightly coloured traditional attire, chattered and laughed, their voices mingling with the lively Afrobeat music.

Garrick surveyed the room, taking in the elaborate decorations - towering floral arrangements, shimmering gold and white fabrics draped from the ceiling, and the tantalizing aroma of Nigerian cuisine wafting from the buffet. His stomach rumbled in anticipation.

"I have to hand it to them," he said, leaning closer to a drunk Harry Lord so that he could be heard over the music, "they know how to throw a party."

Harry clinked David's pint glass. "Nigerians don't do anything halfway. Especially not weddings. Then add on the fact that Chib is a control freak... this is brilliant!"

Garrick couldn't help but feel a pang of envy. He had debated with himself if he should propose to Wendy, now that they were having a child together, but he had never quite been able to justify it. Now, surrounded by so much love and happiness he wondered if he was missing out on something special.

As Garrick stumbled towards the bar, a booming voice cut through his musings. "Garrick, you old bastard!" He turned to see DCI Oliver Kane, looking rather dashing in his own deep crimson agbada, a stark contrast to his usual drab suit. "Can you believe this spread? I've never seen so much food in my life!" He held something up in his hand and took a bite. "I have no idea what this is, but it's delicious!"

DCI Kane was the MET police officer who was tasked to investigate Garrick himself. He was the man responsible for embedding Chib in the Kent team to spy on him. Garrick and Chib had bonded to the point he had asked her to stay even when her duplicity was exposed. With Kane, an uneasy alliance of sorts had kept the two men connected once Garrick's innocence had been proven. Garrick convinced himself that Kane was just doing his job. Garrick's therapist was convinced he was still harbouring bitterness towards the MET detective.

Garrick chuckled. "Better pace yourself, Kane. I don't fancy rolling you out of here at the end of the night."

Kane joined him at the bar, and they watched Garrick's team and members of Chib's old London unit dancing together.

"This is what makes it all worthwhile, eh?" said Kane. "And I hear you're going to be a dad?"

Garrick shot him a look. "Still spying on me?"

Kane chuckled and waved to the barmaid. "I'll get this round to celebrate you."

"It's a free bar."

"My life keeps getting better."

The night progressed in a blur which ended with Chib dragging him to the dance floor. He felt ridiculous, his limbs moving awkwardly to the unfamiliar beat, but as he looked around, he realized nobody was paying him any mind. Everyone was lost in the music, their faces alight with pure, unbridled joy.

Embracing the rest of his team, they danced for what felt like hours, the music never seeming to end. Garrick found himself laughing, really laughing, for the first time in ages. The stress of the job, the weight of his past, all seemed to melt away in the face of this simple, profound happiness. It became a blur, but it was a hungover memory of all their smiling faces, and at one point, Fanta Liu laughing so hard she was in tears.

And returning to Wendy's heavily sleeping form had been the icing on the cake.

Chapter Three

No sooner had he been back in the office with the entire team than he remembered Chib was due to take her delayed honeymoon to the Maldives, if only the passport office would hurry up processing her renewal. Garrick felt yet another sharp pang of jealousy. It was a destination he had thought about going to for its spectacular beaches and the chance to turn his hand back to a spot of diving, in some of the most pristine waters in the world. But it was prohibitively expensive, especially shackled with his new family commitments.

He had scheduled the day after Chib's wedding as a holiday, as she had wisely done, but due to ongoing budgetary restrictions, Superintendent Malcolm Reynolds had summoned him in with a new case. Garrick had been combating a fierce hangover, but it was either tackle an Ikea instruction manual or visit a crime scene and hope to claim the day off later in the week when he didn't feel so terrible.

. . .

Drizzle was so relentless it seeped into every open pocket and seam in Garrick's Barbour jacket. He pulled his hood tighter over his head, but his brow and cheeks were already stinging and damp from the cold spray coming in from the sea. Pebbles crunched underfoot as he and DC Fanta Liu made their way across Samphire Hoe towards the knot of police officers who were all hunched over in their weather-proofs with their backs to the wind. Beyond, brown waves from the English Channel crashed against the shingle shoreline and visibility faded after about 500 yards.

Samphire Hoe was a relatively new piece of UK territory. It was a country park that had been constructed using the waste extracted by digging the Channel Tunnel. 4.9 million cubic metres of soil had formed the idyllic natural reserve, nestled at the foot of the White Cliffs of Dover. It was a pleasant place for a summer walk, but now, at the end of summer, it was the site of something grim.

The officers were clustered round a body which lay face-up on the shore. Garrick was hardened to standing around corpses, but the smell from this one was a tad too pungent. Luckily, the scent of salt spray kept the lingering odour at bay. He crouched down while Fanta remained standing. Her expression was quizzical. When he had first met her, she hadn't reacted too well around corpses, but now she was regarding them like it was just another day in the office.

"Who found her, sir?" Garrick asked the nearest officer, who had his hands stuffed in his jacket pockets for warmth.

"A dog walker," said the officer. "She said she had come this way last night to the beach, but hadn't seen anything. First thing this morning, her dog went nuts. She thought it was a seal or a dolphin, they occasionally wash up along here. But then realised it was more likely another immigrant."

Illegal immigration was a hot topic, none more so than in Kent. At just 20 miles across the Channel from the *Pas-de-Calais* region of France, it was a favourite launch pad for gangs who illegally ferried immigrants across. But the officer clearly hadn't paid too much attention to the body.

It was a woman, wearing a red and grey Berghaus waterproof jacket and jeans. She was barefoot, but the state of her manicured nails and quality of clothing suggested she wasn't an immigrant trying to make her fortune in a country that didn't want her. The body was about six feet up from the water's edge, lying on a bed of seaweed, plastic flotsam and jetsam that had been deposited there during high tide.

"What are your thoughts, Fanta?"

Fanta slowly circled the body, the officers moving further back to allow her in. She finally knelt to get a closer look at the woman's head.

"Well, from her clothes and hairstyle, and those plucked eyebrows, I'm guessing she's wealthy, or middle class. More likely she was walking along the beach and attacked." Fanta pointed to the woman's right hand. "Her middle and little fingernails are broken - I'd suggest she was in a bit of a struggle, whether with someone... or maybe a wave snatched her out into the water if she was walking too close to the edge and clawing at the pebbles. It could be an accident." She shook her head, unable to determine which hypothesis was more likely. "And obviously she hasn't been here for some time." She pulled a face, indicating the more gruesome part of the discovery. "Her left eye is missing, and from the claw marks on her face, looks like seagulls have been pecking at the cadaver before it was found. I think if that was more than a morning's work, the body would have been pecked to death."

Siren's Call

Garrick nodded in agreement, and felt a little flicker of pride that Fanta had come on so well under his mentorship. "I agree with that. Probably drowned then washed up on the beach this morning. Let's get a weather report, see what the water conditions were like last night."

"Look at the back of her head, guv," Fanta said, leaning down so low she used her hands to support herself as she searched for a better angle without moving the body.

Garrick moved round for a better view. The woman's hair and crumpled hood concealed the wound, but congealed blood and matter tangled a patch of hair at the back of her head.

"A clonk on the back of the noggin'," Garrick said pointedly. Two options presented themselves - the more innocent one, that she had been on a boat, fallen and struck her head, perhaps rendering her unconscious, then drowned. The second was the more nefarious idea. That this was murder.

Garrick stood up, unable to prevent a wheeze of exertion escaping his lips as his knees cracked. "We'll have to see what forensics say," he said, looking up and down the beach.

Beaches were notoriously difficult crime scenes. Exposed to the elements, the sea dragged away whatever evidence it could, while the wind eroded crucial telltale signs. It was one of the better places to reduce a killer's risk of being caught.

He found his gaze lingering on the waves as they crashed against the shore, invoking sudden memories of his sister plummeting to her death off a cliff. She had been the architect of a twisted one-sided sibling feud, fuelled by her broken mind. For the past few months, his therapist had painlessly shunted such memories into a dark vault he had no wish to access. But here on the beach, the pounding waves and sharp salty breeze brought it all back with crushing force.

A strong gust of wind took his breath and for several moments he didn't breathe. Fanta gently squeezed his arm, bringing him back to the moment. "Sir, are you okay?" she said in a low voice so the uniforms couldn't hear.

Garrick snapped back to the moment and nodded. "Yeah, Fanta, thanks. Just for a minute there, you know..." He trailed off.

Fanta nodded. The whole team were more than aware now of their boss's terrible past, and not one of them had pressed to ask any further questions, even though events had deeply affected all their lives.

Garrick preferred to keep it that way. He pulled himself together. "So, forensics?" His mind was wandering a little too much to concentrate.

"On the way, sir," Fanta said smartly. She looked around the beach. "I don't think there's much more we can do here without keeping the public away."

Garrick nodded and looked back at the corpse. It was always a sad moment for him, wondering what future life had been snatched from the mystery woman. He gave a long sigh.

"You know what, Fanta? I think there's a caf not too far away." He tilted his head towards the car park. "I suggest we grab a cuppa, warm up, then talk to the dog walker."

"Sounds like a plan I can get on board with," said Fanta, smiling.

The greasy spoon cafe was everything Garrick hoped it would be, from the oversized plastic tomato sauce bottle on the table through to the smell of grease imprinted on the walls. After being ostensibly good with his food choices over

Siren's Call

the last couple of months, mindful he wanted to remain healthy into fatherhood, Wendy had put them both on a strict nutritional diet. Although, being pregnant, she regularly craved the very foods she banned him from eating.

Now, in front of Fanta, he was demolishing a huge plate of an all-day English breakfast, with extra mushrooms spilling into the fried tomatoes, an overly large sausage bleeding fat onto the plate and smothered in baked beans, garnished to the side by two fried eggs and, in his opinion, the intruder in the mix, two hash browns, which were more American. He'd forgone the black pudding as a concession to Wendy, not that she would ever hear that he'd gorged on this delicious feast. He'd even extended to a hot cup of milky tea, which was the perfect accompaniment to the dish. His stomach couldn't handle coffee, but better than a fine wine, the tea was the perfect complement to an English breakfast.

Fanta watched with a mix of disgust and disbelief as Garrick mopped up the stray concoction of beans and egg with a folded triangular piece of brown toast. She'd ordered a cheese toastie and was slowly nibbling through it.

"So, this is turning into your pre-fatherhood vice," she said, eyes darting to his plate.

"Yeah, Wendy's very militant when it comes to keeping me alive. So, this will be our little secret, eh?" Fanta nodded, but looked distracted. "What's on your mind? Did you like it better when I was away from the office?" The smile that flashed across her face was forged. "What is it, Fanta?"

"I was thinking about a promotion." She looked sheepishly away.

Detective Constable Fanta Liu She a relatively new officer, and in the force, everyone had to pay their dues at the coalface before any signs of promotion were granted.

However, she had been involved in several high-profile cases, and Garrick had officially mentioned Fanta's performance above and beyond the call of duty, which had been acknowledged, if not with any honorific title, and certainly not with any financial reward, but she'd gained a certificate in honour of risking her life for the greater good. When Garrick thought about it like that, he didn't blame her for wanting to be fast-tracked to promotion.

She knew all of this, of course, but Garrick also knew with such an exemplary record, Fanta was exactly the type of woman who would start breaking the norms when it came to promotion.

"Do you have anywhere in mind?" he said as nonchalantly as possible.

"There was one in Manchester possibly coming up. And I just heard, there's another one in London that I might be suited for." She gave a sideways glance, obviously embarrassed by sharing her idea of leaving the team.

Garrick looked at his food, feeling that looking directly at her would make her feel even more guilty. He had vague memories of DCI Kane and Fanta talking at Chib's wedding. He wouldn't be surprised if his arch-nemesis was trying to poach his crew.

"I get it, Fanta. I mean, I hope it's nothing to do with how you've been treated here?"

He was surprised when Fanta chuckled. "You mean almost dying on a monthly basis? Nah." Luckily, she was teasing him. "It's not that at all. I mean, I could say a lot of complimentary things about working with you, but that's not my style. And you'll probably think I'm buttering you up to get a good appraisal."

"That's exactly what you are doing, isn't it?"

Fanta nodded. "Well, yeah, but I don't want you to *know* that."

"I'll try to forget."

"That would be appreciated."

A loaded silence fell between the two as Garrick hungrily polished off the food. Eventually, Garrick reluctantly reached an internal decision. "Well, I can't blame you for trying to achieve your very best potential," he said. "If life's taught me one thing, it's don't let any opportunity pass you by. You never know where it's going to lead. And you never know how much time we have for chasing our dreams."

He met Fanta's gaze, which she could only hold for a few seconds before looking away guiltily. "I don't want you to think I'm being disloyal. Or unappreciative. I really enjoyed almost being blown apart when we broke into that house."

Garrick felt on safer ground with Fanta's irony bubbling to the surface.

"It's not about loyalty. It's about ambition. It's about skill." After a thoughtful moment, he added a third caveat that surprised even himself, "And it's about being happy. Don't get me wrong, I'm going to be furious if you leave me in a lurch." He wiped his mouth with a napkin. "But I'd be a complete dick if I wasn't going to support you every step of the way." He gave her a reassuring smile and glanced at his now-battered Guess diver's watch. It sported an inner ring, and after all the time he'd had it, and despite the constant action it had seen, he felt it was the one stylish thing he owned. Although he suspected the battery was going as it kept losing time. "Right, we better get cracking."

. . .

Kirstie Ford lived several miles from the coast, in a little nondescript village of Alkam. She owned in a small bungalow, constructed from ugly modern orange bricks. Large yucca plants the size of Garrick stood as sentinels in the garden, artfully arranged with cacti that lent the entire street a more Mediterranean vibe. With this part of the country increasingly experiencing its own microclimate, the hint of the tropics fitted well.

Before they were halfway up the drive, they could hear the bassy sounds of a dog barking. Kirstie was a 40-year-old woman with a spinster's complexion which she embraced with long prematurely grey-white hair, which was tied back in a ponytail. Despite her grisly find on the beach, she was upbeat with the calmness of a librarian.

She led the detectives into her kitchen and made them both a cup of coffee without even asking. A large dog had bounded to greet them the moment they entered.

"This is Shep. He found the body."

It was some sort of Labrador cross, with a lolling tongue and drool that glued together everything it touched. It made an immediate nosedive for Garrick's groin. After embarrassingly nudging the dog away, and Kirstie doing little to restrain it, Shep's boundless excitement finally eased, and he lay on the coconut coir kitchen mat, chewing on his favourite half-crushed tennis ball.

"I wasn't even going to go out this morning," Kirstie said with a shudder as she recalled events. "Shep gets restless if he doesn't have his morning walk, but the weather had been rotten all night, and it felt just like one of those days when you didn't want to get out of bed."

As was increasingly common, Kirstie worked half her time from home. She was a HR officer for an insurance company and accessed the remote systems via a computer and Zoomed in for the more important meetings. She was obviously happy with this arrangement, and she struck Garrick as a calm person, satisfied with her lot in life. In other words, a reliable witness.

"We normally go down to the beach there as it's often quiet in the morning." As a privately held country park, it was subject to opening times, and only the keenest of ramblers made it for the 7 am opening. She stirred her coffee thoughtfully. Fanta gripped hers with both hands to warm her fingers. Garrick hadn't even touched his cup.

"I always let Shep off his lead. He likes a good run and loves popping in and out of the waves. This morning, the water was a bit choppy. It was drizzly. It wasn't the most pleasant of morning walks." She looked lovingly at her dog. "Like I told the officer, I was listening to my audiobook." She looked askance at Fanta, who was jotting down the odd note. "It was a new John Grisham I'd downloaded. Anyway, I saw that Shep was barking at something on the beach. I didn't think much of it, as we get the occasional seal in this weather, and all sorts of things get washed up. My first instinct was it was somebody else's dog. Last thing you want is a fight on the beach, so I popped out my headphones and shouted to him. Visibility was a bit misty, so I didn't want him to go far. By the time I came closer, it was obviously a person."

She lapsed into silence, her mouth and features tightening in sorrow. She gave a little sniff. "I'm sorry, I've never really seen a dead person before. It sort of puts things in perspective."

The detectives remained tactfully silent as it was turning into an unusual philosophical morning for them. Garrick certainly agreed - no matter how many bodies you saw, it was always the emotional punch, more than the nightmarish visuals, that lingered.

Kirstie sipped her drink. "I put Shep straight back onto his lead and called the police. I just had to linger back and wait, so kept my distance." She gave a shrug. "That's about all there is to it. Do you know who it was?"

"We haven't made a formal ID," Garrick said softly.

"When you were in the car park, were there any other vehicles? People? Did you see anybody else around?"

Kirstie gave it some thought. "No, it was quiet like I said. If there was anyone around, Shep likes to bark at them. You've seen what he's like. We didn't notice anybody."

"Can you confirm the time you found the body?"

"Well, I rang you lot straight away, so by the time that call came in it was probably about 7:20."

Garrick nodded. That tied in with the information he already had.

"Out of curiosity," Fanta suddenly said, "when you were waiting for the police, did the weather get better or worse?"

"It improved a lot. When we found the... person, the waves were really crashing in. By the time the police arrived, the tide had gone out a little bit, and the wind had eased up."

"So, it was high tide?" Fanta asked.

Kirstie nodded. "I suppose so, yeah."

Garrick turned his untouched cup of coffee in a circle to at least give the illusion he was drinking it. As was usually the case with such incidents, there was only so much detail a witness could recall, and she'd been very clear there'd been nobody around. He was about to wind up the interview, but something was on Fanta's mind.

"When you were walking along and you noticed Shep barking, was he barking at the body?"

Kirstie was about to nod, then looked at her dog. "Well, I suppose... yeah, but..." She frowned, thinking about it. "He was barking out at the water, probably excited by the waves."

Fanta nodded and made a note. Garrick looked at her quizzically, wondering where she was going with that line of questioning.

"And you were listening to your new Grisham, but when you pulled your headphones out, could you hear anything?"

Again, Kirstie was silent for a moment as she pulled a face, not entirely sure of her own answer. "It was windy, and I had my hood up, but now you mention it, maybe..." She frowned. "Maybe there could have been a bit of an engine sound. But I could just be imagining that."

Chapter Four

Before the coroner got in touch with the investigation team to deliver their verdict on the deceased, little progress had been made on identification. The woman hadn't been found with any personal possessions, and the missing persons database hadn't provided a result. She was officially a Jane Doe.

As Garrick's team had experience dealing with immigrants illegally trying to enter the country on previous cases, DC Harry Lord had reached out to their counterparts in France, particularly in the Pas-de-Calais region directly opposite where the body was found. He extended inquiries to the notorious *Sangatte* camp where people fleeing persecution and seeking a better life found themselves in unsanitary and dire conditions. The French authorities had since closed it, although various *jungles* routinely appeared, with numbers swelling to 500 occupants - only to be shut down by authorities when the political climate forced them to act.

DS Okon had expressed her doubts about that avenue of investigation. When considering the deceased's clothes and apparent personal care, she didn't think the woman fitted that narrative. She suspected she was part of the affluent community of yacht owners that used Kent's harbours.

Garrick was beginning to worry that this would just be another one of those leadless cases that grow cold and slip into the archives, never to be solved. It was an open wound for law enforcement that there were many more of those cases.

He and Chib turned up at the coroner's office in Canterbury. It was a plain-looking building which he had attended many times before, never in much of a rush to visit again. While a crime scene held the promise of intrigue despite the gruesome situation, the cold slabs of a pathology office lacked any such sense of mystery. They were a harsh reminder of a person's mortality.

Garrick shook his head, trying to dislodge the negative thoughts. Like all good coppers, soldiers and medical practitioners, feelings and emotions had no part to play while on duty. The ability to separate work from their personal lives was essential to stay sane. He was due a therapy session with his new psychologist. It had been going well, and he was able to detach recent hardships from his present circumstances, although there was still a melancholy cloud smothering his thoughts. The shrink hadn't suggested the cause, but Garrick was starting to draw parallels with the increasing baby talk with Wendy. He was beginning to wonder if he wasn't equipped for fatherhood and the thought of bringing an innocent new life into such a harsh world was a mistake, especially when he didn't think he could possibly be a good father. He'd be a disappointment, like his old man. He knew postnatal depression was a worryingly real condition, but he was pretty certain there was no such thing as pre-paternal gloom.

He tried to distract himself, listening to Chib talk about problems with the passport office processing her renewal, and it threatened the long-delayed honeymoon which was rapidly coming up. As they pulled into the car park, the conversation naturally shifted gear to Fanta's proposed job search.

"I mean, she's already packed in a lot of experience, more than I had when I took the role," said Chib with a casual shrug. She glanced at Garrick. "And if she doesn't go elsewhere, then it'll be my job she'd be eyeing. And I like my job."

It was, of course, a playful comment, but it made Garrick wonder if there was any tension there, considering Chib's chequered history regarding how she arrived on the team. It was still something raw amongst them, although it was never mentioned.

"So, you think it's a good idea?" Garrick asked. "I'd already said she has my blessing, although I'm not sure if I actually meant it."

Chib gave a wistful smile. "The alternative is giving her static and not supporting her, which means she'd just resent being stuck with us."

"Damned if I do. Damned if I don't."

They signed into the coroner's office after presenting their ID cards, despite the receptionist knowing them well enough by now. Dr Spackman, a middle-aged pathologist, sporting thick-framed black glasses that magnified his eyes, and neatly groomed greying stubble, greeted them. Garrick had dealt with him before, although he wasn't sure if the doctor recognised him. He was certainly a man of few words, who had condensed the art of conversation into mere punctuated sentences.

Spackman indicated a set of scrubs in the locker room, then showed them through to the theatre beyond. Once covered by the protective scrubs, and hands vigorously washed to prevent infection, they entered the brightly lit theatre which was as cool as ever. The woman's body was presented on the table covered head-to-toe by a dark blue sheet. Without preamble, Dr Spackman drew back the cover and used a metal rod to point under the woman's neck. Chib hurried to extract her pen and pad to take notes, but he had already started his summary.

"There is evidence of blunt force trauma just here in the cranium, with vertebrae C_5 and C_6 shattered. Several inches further down, her left clavicle was fractured from another blow." He moved the rod diagonally across the front of her body to indicate the relationship between the wounds. "It was the same blow to the back that caused this."

"Did that kill her?" Chib asked.

The doctor shook his head. "No, she drowned. With this kind of injury, I suspect she was alive – awake, conscious, but perhaps too dazed to react to save herself. A broken clavicle would have massively reduced mobility in her arm. So even if she was a good swimmer, she was possibly too weak to swim."

Garrick nodded; his eyes drawn to the woman's hands. As Fanta had pointed out, her manicured fingernails were broken.

"Any signs of a struggle or restraint?"

The doctor followed his gaze and indicated the broken nails on both hands. "This suggests she was scrambling on something, trying to save herself." With his latex-gloved hands, he gently raised her right hand and indicated the detectives should move closer. "Just under here you see traces of blue paint." Sure enough, tiny flecks of dried blue paint were lodged millimetres under the nail. "I've sent some for analysis, but I imagine that's from a boat."

Chib nodded and cocked her head as she tried to imagine the woman's last moments. "So, she was struck from behind, fell overboard, and maybe was grasping at the side to pull herself up?"

Dr Spackman nodded. "That's as good a conjecture as any."

"The question is – was it murder?"

The doctor pulled an indecisive face. "I've seen injuries like this in reports, particularly on yachts and sailing ships when somebody has been hit by a boom and tossed overboard."

Chib looked surprised. "Are you saying that she could have been on her own?"

"I can't rule it out. This could be nothing more than a tragic accident. Of course, then you'd need to find the boat. It could have run aground anywhere, or sunk, or still be sailing out there."

"Or stolen," Garrick said almost dismissively, feeling a little irritated, hoping to have some solid evidence pointing in one direction – towards an accident or premeditated murder. "Anything else you can give us on the cause of death?"

"On the cause of death? No. She was *relatively* healthy, considering." He waved the rod towards her mouth. "Healthy teeth. She looked after herself." He moved the sheet further down, being tactful enough to just cover her pubic area as he pointed to the ghost of a scar on her lower right abdomen. "She'd had her appendix out, some years ago."

Siren's Call

The doctor then pointed to her ears. "She has a double piercing on both earlobes." Garrick angled himself to look and noticed there was no jewellery embedded there. "And on the left ear, she has a piercing in the upper lobe." There was a small metal circle still anchored in place.

Garrick felt somewhat relieved. The piercings and scar were handy identifiable features. Now all that remained was getting the message out that this woman had died. That was difficult enough, with only the local online media available, which meant it would just be on an easily ignorable website alongside so many other missing people reported every month. It may come down to a matter of luck to identify her.

"She had been wearing make-up," Dr Spackman added. "The saltwater had scoured most of it off, but there are still faint traces of lipstick and a bit of eyeshadow."

The doctor hesitated and Garrick's mind raced back to something he had said.

"Why did you say she was 'relatively healthy, considering'? Considering what?"

Spackman moved the sheet to cover the appendix scar, and angled the body to reveal an ugly red gash on her back.

"A stab wound?"

"She'd had an operation. A new kidney. And recently. Within days."

"That should be easy to find on the records," said Chib.

Garrick wasn't convinced. "If it happened here. If it was on the continent…"

"It looks like a professional job, but why any hospital would discharge her so quickly is beyond me. After such major surgery, she should not have been travelling in a car, let alone a boat."

. . .

The detectives thanked Spackman and left. Garrick had attended many autopsies without issue, yet he found himself sucking in a deep breath outside in the fresh air. He wasn't normally prone to feeling anxious, and wondered if it was some holdover from the recent barrage of dreadful personal experiences.

Chib flicked through her notes which, as ever, had been written in perfect cursive in her notebook. "I'd pin her age somewhere in her thirties. It doesn't feel as if this was just some boating accident?"

"No way. This stinks of a kidnapping, or she was fleeing for her life."

"If she was on a boat on her own, in that weather...I think it's more likely it would have washed ashore too, not floated back out to sea. And I'm no sailor, but I doubt it was quite rough enough to sink a seaworthy boat."

"If she was on a boat alone, doesn't that suggest a degree of sailing competency? And if she's competent, she wouldn't have gone out in a storm."

They reached the detectives' pool car, and Garrick tossed the keys over to Chib.

"Didn't you say the witness said she heard an engine? It was misty."

"She *thought* she heard it. But was doubtful. Fanta led her on that question. I think she was just responding naturally. Trying to please us."

Witness statements were notoriously unreliable. Descriptions often didn't match and even the colours of clothing could be wildly inaccurate. David and Wendy had taken up Friday evenings watching a quiz show on Channel 4: *I Literally Just Told You*, in which comedian Jimmy Carr asked questions about events that had only occurred moments earlier, and they often struggled to answer correctly. Garrick thought it was a perfect representation of witness behaviour.

"Of course, we forget the other possibility," said Chib as they sat inside the car. Garrick prompted her with a nod. "That she was on a boat moored to the shore and fell in that way. In one case she was travelling here, in the other, out towards France."

Garrick opened his mouth to flippantly cast the idea aside, but the possibility had taken seed.

"Where's the nearest marina to where the body was found?"

Chib started the engine. "You've got sat-nav on your phone, haven't you, Guv? Why don't you tell me where we're going next?"

There were three marinas, the nearest being Dover Harbour itself. Being so busy, and under the nose of Border Force and the police, Garrick ruled it out, so they requested uniformed officers to make enquiries there. Folkestone Boat Dock was the nearest to the east, but that was overlooked by tourists and day-trippers walking along the waterfront. Garrick's gut was telling him Sandwich Marina, which lay beyond Dover and on the edge of the North Sea proper, was a more likely candidate.

By the time they arrived, there was a brisk breeze, but the sky was sapphire blue. Seagulls buzzed and circled over the water, keeping a beady eye on a pair of fishermen at the end of a short pier. The marina itself sat on the River Stour, with a pleasant thirty-minute ride to the tidal estuary of Pegwell Bay. It was a small, busy operation that provided servicing, and lacked the glamour Garrick expected from owning a boat.

There was a range of boats, from small fishing vessels to more upmarket yachts, all of which were in the dry-dock area being serviced or stored. Others sat out on the river, moored to the bank. The two detectives circled the marina, looking for something with a mast, particularly one with a chunky boom that could have clobbered the woman into the water. While there were a couple of possible contenders, one with a grey hull, one red, they didn't sport the blue paintwork Spackman had found under Jane Doe's fingernails. It had been a punt, but Garrick realised they could spend all their time strolling through marinas and never come across the boat. Chib suggested they return to the station and log their findings into the HOLMES database. As they walked back to the car, Garrick's eyes strayed to the fishermen. His old skills, nurtured from pounding the streets as a uniformed officer, made him raise his hand to signal for their attention.

"You know what, Chib? Never underestimate the power of local knowledge." He veered towards the fishermen.

The two men were in their fifties. The larger of the two, who would charitably be termed 'plus-sized' these days or, at the very least, on Garrick's report he would be noted as having a 'ruddy complexion', sported a large bald patch. The other man, edging much more towards sixty with sallow cheeks and a scraggly grey beard, shared a can of Stella between them, with another two already crushed to the side. They sat on plastic tackle boxes, thick all-weather coats unzipped to reveal old, hole-riddled cardigans underneath.

"Afternoon, lads," Garrick said amiably.

In turn, the men gave him a vacant look and a salty nod.

"Caught much?"

Siren's Call

"Nah," said the larger man. "Bit dead today. You sometimes get that after a storm. Could go either way. Today, I think it's buggered up my chances of a fish supper."

The thin guy hawked in his throat, summoning up a ball of phlegm which he then spat into the water. Garrick wondered if it was that, rather than the storm, which scared the fish away.

"I was just wondering if you lads have seen any boats coming in or out over the last few days? A blue one in particular. Or one with at least with some blue on it."

The large man laughed, took a swig of beer. "A blue one? Now you're getting specific, mate. What do you think, Captain Birdseye? Seen any blue boats?"

His thinner companion gave a gruff laugh and hawked again into the water.

"I'm just curious," Garrick replied with a smile.

The big man looked at him, eyes narrowing. "You a copper?"

Garrick gave a wry smile. "A really bad undercover one."

That provoked a snicker from the man. He relaxed now that the rules were established. "Not been much going in or out this morning, to be honest. And we've been here yesterday. Not much then, either. Not really the weather for it. You lookin' for smugglers?"

"Could be," said Garrick. He glanced at a bewildered Chib.

The thinner man gave a thoughtful murmur. "You know, every now and again you see those boats running in, people trying to cross over. If I can sit on the beach and spot 'em, why isn't the Navy doing anything about 'em?"

Garrick braced himself for an outburst. He really didn't

want to have a conversation about the rights and wrongs of immigration.

The man continued, wiping his running nose with the back of his hand. "I mean, you'd think the Navy or Coastguard would see 'em coming and help the poor sods."

Pleasantly surprised, Garrick couldn't help but mutter in agreement.

"It's not their fault," the man continued with more authority. "I wouldn't want to come over here from a lovely sunny country unless I had to." He looked Garrick directly in the eye. "If you're asking if I've seen any of 'em – no. And even if I did, I don't think I'd want to grass 'em up."

"Fair enough," Garrick said. "But don't they cross in dinghies and rubber boats?"

The man looked thoughtful. "Aye. They cross in anything they can get their hands on, usually. So, if you're looking for something a bit smarter, I'd be looking for another culprit."

"Smugglers?"

The man's eyes darted around. "They don't all belong in old books. People smuggle anythin' these days."

Garrick thanked the men, and he and Chib returned to their car.

"Wow. Local knowledge..." she mocked.

"Well, it certainly errs on the side that she wasn't sneaking into the country," he said defensively. "Which raises the issue of why she was on a boat in the first place. And to me, I'm starting to think her identity is a little bit more homegrown."

Chapter Five

As a detective, Garrick embraced puzzles and was quite proud of the logical way he could slot life together to reveal a deeper, often secret, truth. This is why he found himself lying on the floor in the small upstairs second bedroom of the cramped property he rented with Wendy.

He was beginning to wonder what the Swedes had ever done to him. Trying to assemble the Malmö cupboard should, on the face of it, be a straightforward proposition. He didn't consider himself a competent handyman, but the instructions were crystal clear. However, the physical rendition of his efforts told another tale that M.C. Escher would approve of.

He'd spent the previous evening applying green paint to the room, a colour both he and Wendy had agreed on, in lieu of a more traditional pink. Not that Garrick was a stickler for tradition; he had just assumed Wendy was. The light green paint made the room feel fresher and larger, so he couldn't quibble. The assembly of the furniture, though, had become a nightmare—a task consigned to him when he'd finally got home from work.

With the possible homicide case, activity in the office had stepped up, but as it was still early days in the investigation period, there was no need to pull in overtime. And with Wendy weeks away from delivery, he suddenly felt time was conspiring against him.

The previous day, he'd had his scheduled appointment with his therapist, which had been a light and breezy affair. So, despite the logistical problem, Wendy's ballooning stomach, and an active murder investigation, Garrick felt surprisingly relaxed and in fine spirits.

He twisted the Allen key, gripped painfully between his thumb and index finger, and sucked in a deep breath, resisting the urge to hurl the section of MDF out of the window. The key refused to move, so he threw that across the room instead. He realised that he'd have to backtrack several steps, unscrewing screws and unbolting bolts until he was back to component parts to start again. The thought of it brought an unexpected smile to his face. In some deep recess of his mind, he wondered if he'd deliberately made the mistakes just so he could spend more time on the assembly. He was starting to view Ikea as an analogy for his life, for life. Things can be put together incorrectly and cause situations not to work, but steps can be taken to remedy the harm, and life could be reassembled into the perfect Malmö, or as he was viewing it, into a very steady life with Wendy and their daughter. It was moments like this that chased away the paternal blues that had been threatening him.

This wasn't a life he'd planned. If he was honest, other than regular dating, it wasn't a life he'd perceived that he needed, and an inner part of him was still battling the true responsibilities of adulthood. Despite being middle-aged, his therapist had assured him that feeling anxious about fatherhood was natural, as it signalled a major change in his lifestyle. But, despite the stresses, it shouldn't be seen as a negative one.

He hadn't shared his emotional rollercoaster with Wendy, partly because he thought it was unfair to burden her with his own problems when she was in clear physical discomfort, but mostly because he didn't want her to think badly of him. From the moment they first dated, there had been an incident in the news which had thrust him into the limelight and made him something of a celebrity hero, at least in her eyes. And after everything they'd been through, he could still take that positive from all the gloom they had endured. She had come to know him so well. Better than he knew himself.

When he got home the previous night, he was in a foul mood. He was surprised to see his old fossil kit had been laid out on the table after it had been packed into a box he'd thrown into a corner after he'd sold his old house. He hadn't really thought about it for a long while, but seeing the fragments of rock laid out on a light green fluffy felt sheet slowly brought back the lost feelings he experienced when carving away stone to reveal the prehistoric treasures within. He'd built up quite a collection of ancient snail shells, shark's teeth, and the odd fragment of bone from the beaches around Kent, all of which he'd carefully carved out of the stone. Aside from his interest in dinosaurs, he'd found the slow, delicate clearing of sediment from bone or cartilage to be a zen-like experience. Better than yoga, which he had stopped doing since returning to work.

Wendy had evidently thought that his hobby was missing

from his life. In an odd way, the moment he'd started up the drill, with the TV murmuring in the background and Wendy giving the occasional snore from the couch, it felt like a moment of completion. His old self slowly rising to the surface.

However, another spectre was rising behind him, and for that, he blamed Chib. Her wedding had affected him in a way he never thought it would, and now he was wondering how he and Wendy should further evolve. Marriage had been a topic to tiptoe around, second only to children. And look how that had turned out.

He licked his lips, retrieved the Allen key from the corner of the room, and began dismantling the furniture in an act that felt as if he was stripping away the layers of his life and the self-imposed barriers he'd erected as he'd grown up. These barriers had prevented him from blossoming as a person, and more than ever, he felt as if he was lacking a sense of family in his life. He all but had none of his own.

Garrick's mind wandered, and his attention drifted from the pictogram instructions on the floor next to him. His hands moved of their own volition as the furniture came together, allowing his mind to run free around abstract thoughts.

His team had become his family. And like any family, there was bickering, rivalries, and jealousies. But they had been through thick and thin and supported one another with their lives. They'd all borne scars from the crimes they'd solved. Fanta had nearly been killed in a booby trap explosion. Harry Lord sported a permanent limp after being run down by a suspect. Wilkes and Chib bore the personal mental scars of battle, and Garrick had been punched black and blue from the craziness that had befallen him.

It was through the haze of these blurring thoughts that he finally realised he was tightening the last screw of the wardrobe door. He hadn't glanced at the instructions at all, and as he stepped back, he felt a wave of satisfaction that it looked exactly like it should in the picture. The fact that there appeared to be three bolts and a washer spare to the side was something he tried to ignore. After all, he was certain they put spare parts in these days anyway. He felt a slight thrill, as he often did when they wrapped up a case. He'd got there in the end. And in some ways, that's all that counted.

Three days after Jane Doe was found on the beach, they were still no clearer about identifying the woman. Missing people reports across the UK revealed no matches, and the French authorities were slow in responding.

Chib waved a hand towards her computer screen and shook her head. "Spackman re-examined the kidney surgery and confirmed it was a professional job, although the scar tissue indicated there may have been a previous attempt, but it's impossible to tell. From the records, it certainly wasn't done on the NHS. And so far, nothing has shown up on private records. But they're slow to come in."

Garrick stood behind her, staring at the email inbox on her screen, the contents of which were reports from various sources confirming they had no idea who the woman was.

"So, all fingers point to her being a foreign national."

"It seems that way. But they're slower as we're waiting for the French."

"Okay, get on to Interpol, their missing persons, and see if that shakes anything up."

"Already plugging away on it, Guv," DC Lord said, his head just visible from behind his monitor.

Chib gave a frustrated sigh. They both knew that was a long process that relied on the efficiency of various nations' police forces, their willingness to spend time searching through records, and a desire to prioritise the search. When combined internationally, it was *marginally* more efficient than finding a needle in a haystack by hand, but only just.

As the story had garnered no press attention, any hope that the woman had any worried neighbours couldn't be explored. Garrick had considered feeding the story to Molly Meyers, the reporter who had become famous from DCI Garrick's cases; he'd saved from a brutal kidnapping, in which she'd lost half a finger, and with whom he'd travelled with to the USA so they could track down his sister's killer. Since those traumatic escapades, Molly had leaped from a local newspaper reporter to the face of BBC Southeast news, to an acclaimed national reporter. Her interest in a possible illegal immigrant who'd fallen off a boat was deemed unworthy for press coverage.

Chib had spat out her feelings on this, pondering how, as a society, they had got to the position that one life was worth more than another.

"We've been here before, and it's an uphill battle," Garrick reminded her. He simply didn't have the energy to argue.

Chib flicked through to another case file from a team in Canterbury. "This detective has been tracking through several human trafficking cases."

She scrolled through the lengthy file, complete with photographs of inflatable rafts that had washed up on the beaches around Kent and dozens of bodies filed over time, virtually all of whom were dark-skinned immigrants fleeing their own countries.

"See if they want to take this off us," Garrick said hopefully, and then instantly felt a pang of regret when she shot him a dark look.

"Passing the buck, are we, Guv?" she said pointedly.

"Not if it helps his case," he said defensively, although she had him, and salted the wound with:

"Not worthy for the news. And not worthy enough for us."

Garrick suddenly felt an overwhelming desire to focus back on the car thief case that the team had been saddled with while he'd been on leave. At least it had some *Fast and Furious* vibes.

"My point," Chib continued, "is that our Jane Doe does not fit the usual pattern of immigrants." She stared challengingly at him.

Garrick knew she was driving at the colour of the woman's skin and apparent social status gleaned from her clothing, so he remained diplomatically silent and simply nodded. He thought back to the two fishermen on the quay and their rather enigmatic comments about smugglers. He was aware that smuggling was a very modern crime, yet he couldn't help but think back to the *Enid Blyton* books he'd read growing up; all romantic tales of friends busting up criminal gangs. He expressed this to Chib, leaving out his childhood reading list.

"You know, that feels like it might make sense."

"Nice to know I'm not running out of fresh ideas, Chib."

"I never say *that*."

"Not to my face, at least."

A broad, sparkling grin broke across Chib's face in a very

clear sign of agreement. Garrick couldn't repress a smile back. He was thankful that his staff took the piss out of him. It made him feel more human in the face of inhumanity.

"Well, with lack of evidence on the beach at the moment, all we can do is hope that an ID on the body comes through sooner rather than later." He glanced around the office. Sean was at his desk and looked very intent considering the lack of work they had to do. Maybe he was searching for another job, too? Lord had disappeared into the kitchen on his regular tea run. "Where's Fanta? Did she come in today?"

"She said she needed to check on something."

"That's so very vague and so very Fanta." Garrick wondered if it was code for *job interview*.

"Well, that is her job, I suppose."

It was around lunchtime when he finally got a call from DC Fanta Liu with an address she wanted them to meet at.

At 1:20 pm Garrick arrived at the Dover Maritime Rescue Coordination Centre building, at St Margaret's at Cliffe. It was operated by HM Coastguard as part of their network of surveillance stations around the UK, always on hand for emergencies, working with the Royal National Lifeboat Institution (RLNI) and the NCI (National Coastwatch Institution), the latter two of which were funded from donations and run by volunteers.

Garrick had never been here before and had always assumed he was persona non grata when it came to the Coastguard after accidentally destroying one of their precious lifeboats in a situation he'd rather forget about.

To his surprise, the Coastguard's Langdon Battery building was an odd-shaped modern structure that looked like an elegant Frank Lloyd Wright design that belonged in California rather than in Kent.

He entered the lobby, which was small, and displayed pictures of various Coastguard vessels on the wall. A rosy-faced, middle-aged receptionist greeted him with a warm smile, announcing that she'd been expecting him, and asked him to sign the visitor's book. He saw that the immediate signature above his was Fanta's.

With him logged safely in, the receptionist's next concern was whether he was hydrated enough and needed a coffee or water. Garrick declined, and she led him through several corridors before knocking on a door and then opening it without waiting for a response. Inside, Garrick had been expecting a large space, with multiple desks and people sitting vigilantly at computer terminals tracking shipping across the busy channel. Instead, it was a small, darkened room, illuminated by four large screens arranged on a single desk. Garrick had been expecting a large, state-of-the-art command centre that belonged in a *Jason Bourne* movie. Instead, he was disappointed. The room gave the appearance of something far less high-tech, as if a bunch of students had decided to make a low-budget version of a Bond command post.

Fanta sat with a smartly dressed officer with salt-and-pepper hair and a crisp white shirt with naval markings on the sleeve.

"Here he is!" she declared with a smile, and she stood, ushering Garrick into her vacated seat. "About time."

The man offered his hand to Garrick but didn't offer a name.

"Detective. Welcome to the Hub."

"I was expecting... more."

An enigmatic smile played on the man's face. "The main centre is there," he pointed upwards. "That's the MRCC. We're here to support the latest Government policies on behalf of Border Force."

"He's with the Navy," Fanta said in a conspiratorially low voice. She nudged the man's shoulder. "Tell him what you told me."

The officer's bemused expression was something that Garrick was all too familiar with from people who'd spent too much time around Fanta. She possessed a likeable enthusiasm that was almost a form of positive bullying. He gestured to the screens.

"This is live tracking data for vessels around the Channel."

Garrick leaned back in the chair and took in the screens.

"So here, we track shipping across the Channel. The data comes from upstairs, but my little task is really to look for what's filtering through that *shouldn't* be there."

Garrick squinted closely at the nearest screen. Basic graphics depicted the coastline, and the water was a mass of white dots with identifying alphanumeric codes.

"Shipping must have a transponder to identify themselves. This is linked to a computer, like a black box on an airplane. On a ship it's called a VDR – Voyage Data Recorder. It stores all the data for each voyage. Those codes are AIS transponders – the Automatic Identification System that identifies each vessel."

"Every boat has them?"

"*Ship*." He caught Garrick's confusion. "Sorry. I'm a Naval guy. Ships float on water, boats go under. Like submarines. And no. They're only required by vessels over 300 tonnes."

"Ah. So smaller ships can't be identified?"

"There are two classes. Class-A are the ones I mentioned. Class-B transponders are used by smaller craft, fishing vessels, yachts, but are not mandatory. And they are low wattage too, so the signal doesn't carry beyond about 10 miles." He used an electronic pen to circle a target on the screen. The identifying data appears on a pop-up window. "Like this one. It's a private launch that set sail from Dunkirk."

"You mean, as busy as this all looks, there are small craft dodging through it all, without transponders?"

"Exactly." He circled another blip on the screen. This time the pop-up window read there was no tracking data. "Radar picks it up, but we have no idea what it is without a visual sighting."

"That's why it's so difficult to track illegal boats," said Fanta.

The Navy man nodded. "And the smaller vessels may not show up on radar either. At least, from our shore-based radar. All this data is managed by CNIS – sorry, the Channel Navigational Information Service base here and," he gestured with a finger, "the CROSS facility in Gris Nez. Out at sea, shipping vessels have sophisticated systems that can pick up the smallest of objects to prevent them from running into some fools floating across on a lilo."

Garrick sat back in his seat. He had anticipated that Fanta had uncovered something that would put the case on track. Instead, he was beginning to realise the futility of searching for a ship at sea that didn't want to be found.

"That's a lot of people potentially running in the dark. And if we're talking about people who don't want to be caught... they can just vanish."

"That is precisely why I'm here. The Channel is one of the busiest shipping lanes in the world. We have about 400 vessels pass through, and those are just the registered shipping, ferries, that sort of thing. It's heavily congested. It's prone to foul weather. In reality, there's not a lot of space. So, when anyone's up to no good, they can switch the transponder off and run dark."

"They call them ghost ships!" Fanta added with a tremor of excitement.

Garrick made a hopeless gesture with his hands. "So what can you do?"

"Like I said, we're looking for what isn't there, but should be. We're looking for holes that other ships are avoiding. You see, we have to run a very tight TSS here." Again, he caught Garrick's blank look. Abbreviations were second nature in the Navy. He clarified: "Traffic Separation System. Basically, keeping everybody in their lanes."

The nature of the man's work began to dawn on Garrick. "You mean, if a ship veers off course to avoid a boat, all you will see is the bigger vessel swerving around an empty space?"

"Exactly." The officer swept his hands across the entire system, presenting it to his audience. "And this uses the very latest artificial intelligence system to identify sudden course corrections, transponders turning on and off, that sort of thing."

Something was bothering Fanta. "If transponders are not legally required, why would people have them to turn off?"

"It provides a good cover. Remember, they don't work well beyond 10 miles. At its narrowest, the Channel is 21 miles. If a boat is ever stopped for an inspection, and it has a transponder, it's less likely to fall under the officer's scrutiny.

And when it vanishes off radar, anything from range to faulty equipment can be used as an excuse. Lucky for me, AI can only analyse the data so far. There is still nothing better than good old human eyeballing. My team are trained in spotting what isn't there."

"Let me guess, you've discovered a ghost ship?"

Fanta shook her head. "No, we've discovered the complete opposite." Garrick frowned, not quite following her logic.

She tapped the Officer on the arm. "Show him."

With a slight sigh of wary tolerance, the officer drew Garrick's gaze to another screen, which showed shipping data.

"Detective Liu here asked me to look at a very specific period of time. This is from two hours before your body's suspected time of death."

Other than the timecodes and a slightly different array of transponders, Garrick couldn't see a difference between the recording and the live screen.

Fanta gave a sudden slight bound in her chair. "Did you see it?"

Garrick shook his head. "What am I looking at?"

Before the Officer could do anything, Fanta intervened and took the mouse from him. She moved the pointer over to a video scroll bar and rewound the time period. Then she circled the mouse over an empty patch of sea. "Look here." She hit play.

Garrick watched as the other transponders all slowly moved - and then suddenly, one dot blinked into existence in the empty area Fanta had circled.

"They turned the transponder on?"

Fanta nodded excitedly. "Exactly!"

"Why?" Intrigued, both he and Fanta drew closer to the screen. "What can you tell us about this boat - *ship*?"

The officer retrieved his mouse from Fanta and clicked through a series of options so quickly Garrick lost track of what was going on. Suddenly, lines appeared, marking the path and final destinations of each transponder. He scrolled along the screen so Garrick could follow the line straight to a patch of beach towards Eastbourne.

"The vessel is registered in Liverpool." He indicated the ID number. "But I have already checked this. It's an old number from a boat that sank three years ago."

"It's been cloned?"

"It looks that way. And this is the path it took. For some reason, they left the transponder on right up until it stopped broadcasting when it came ashore. This was the speed... wow. Fast. Maybe it was a RIB or small speedboat."

Fanta held up her phone, where she already had Google Maps open showing a satellite image of the Pevensey Bay area in East Sussex.

"They came ashore here!" she beamed.

Garrick felt a flood of relief that they may finally have a breakthrough, even if it was in the neighbouring country of East Sussex. He was looking forward to a trip across county lines to see what, exactly, had arrived on that beach.

Chapter Six

Although only fifteen miles as the crow flies, it took Garrick and Fanta almost an hour and a half to reach the beach at Pevensey Bay after driving along a rat's nest of A roads constantly plagued by roadworks, pushing them onto narrow B roads which at times were barely wide enough for the car to pass. As they slowed behind an unhurried tractor, Garrick asked Fanta the question that was gnawing at him.

"Talking to that bloke was a fine bit of detective work, Liu."

"Thank you."

"You're not trying to impress people, are you?"

"Do I still need to impress with my track record?"

Garrick wisely steered the conversation from that path.

"How did you know about him, if that operation is supposed to be a secret?"

Fanta hesitated for a moment, reluctant to give up her coveted sources. She finally broke.

"My brother's in the Navy. Based in Portsmouth."

"You have a brother?" Garrick's surprise amused Fanta.

"The one child policy doesn't apply to all Chinese people."

"I didn't mean..." Garrick trailed off. Putting up with his DC's sarcasm wasn't worth the effort. He had no idea she had a brother. He knew very little about any of his team's lives outside the unit. Why was that only bothering him now?

The section of East Sussex coastline wasn't easily accessible to the public, so Garrick had to park in a lay-by, then the detectives scrambled over wooden fences and across a field. The two figures cut black lines through the vivid yellow rapeseed fields until they reached a fence at the far side, which led to a steep incline down to the shingle beach.

It was a clear day with a brisk breeze blowing across the Channel, gently tossing waves onto the shore. The coastline itself was jagged, zigzagging with plenty of naturally shielded bays. Fanta pulled the collar of her bright red Berghaus coat tighter as she checked the GPS on her phone. There wasn't much of a signal, but fortunately the map still functioned and indicated their destination was to the east.

They walked for several minutes in self-reflective silence before Garrick's attention was drawn to gulls cartwheeling in the air ahead and screaming loudly at one another. The beach's incline sharpened, causing each footfall to sink a little in the fine stones and tilt them both slightly off balance. Garrick could already feel the muscles in his calves complaining. Their natural pacing had already put Fanta several yards ahead as they rounded another crook along the shore. She glanced back at him and gave an encouraging wave to hurry him. Shuffling onwards, Garrick was already out of breath as he joined her.

Siren's Call

"Look!" Fanta said excitedly.

Dragged several yards onto the shingles was a peeling pale-blue wooden fishing boat about thirty foot in length. Tarnished by the wind, it looked as if it had been here some while, although they knew that wasn't the case. Out on the sea, it would look like any other aging fishing launch. They crunched further across the pebbles. As they neared, it became clear that the back of the boat was black and burnt.

"Did the engine catch fire?" Fanta slowly circled around the stern.

The ship had grounded itself prow first and now sat perpendicular to the water. The large outboard engine on the back was twisted and charred, presumably the cause of the fire itself. Flames had spread through the back half of the boat, and the wood was charred and twisted in places, and looked barely watertight.

"That engine looks too big and powerful for a boat like this, don't you think?" said Garrick.

Fanta nodded. "Why put it on a boat that looks as if it's going to fall apart?" She chewed her lip thoughtfully.

"Your pally officer thought it might be a RIB," Garrick said as he mulled his thoughts. "But it's something that moves like the clappers through the water, but looks like a piece of crap on it." He gestured with his hands as if presenting the boat as a prize.

Fanta gave a little "Oh" as she cottoned on to his thoughts. "It's in disguise!"

Garrick nodded. "Like he said, keep the transponder on just long enough to look like a legitimate vessel leaving the port, then run under the radar. If anyone sees it from above it doesn't look like your typical fast-moving boat bringing contraband in. Just some shitty boat out fishing."

"Ship," Fanta corrected him as they walked around the stern.

Garrick studied the water five yards away. He pointed to a line of dark brown seaweed that ran along the coast. "This marks the high tide."

Fanta followed the line of seaweed, which led up to the stern of the boat. "So it was either pulled further ashore at high tide, or it came speeding up here and deliberately beached itself."

"If they had engine problems, maybe that was intentional?"

Having almost completed a full orbit of the vessel, Garrick drew level with a small wooden ladder bolted to the side of the hull to provide access onto the deck. He tested a rung with his foot. It was firm, the wood only painted to look old and distressed. He climbed aboard.

Now level with the small two-metre squared cabin, Garrick remembered the coroner's guess about a sailing boom striking the back of Jane Doe's head. This ship didn't have a mast, so either it was the wrong vehicle, or her vertebrae had been broken some other way. The smell of charred wood was stronger up here. He could see the fire had damaged the deck, and scorched a metal baseball bat that had rolled into the corner. That fitted the bill for a possible weapon.

Fanta sprightly ascended the ladder to join him, and he couldn't help but notice the grin on her face.

"What's up?"

"I like small boats," she admitted. "They're so much fun. Not as good as jet skis, though."

Garrick shuddered and grimaced. Last time they had been on a boat together it had been a heart-stopping experience, almost literally. At least this time it promised to be a calmer affair.

Careful not to touch anything, Garrick peered through the cabin side window. The glass was covered in grime and smothered in fresh layers of bird droppings, so he couldn't see much inside. He moved around to the access door and stopped. Fanta almost walked into him as she checked her balance on the skewed deck. The cabin door was smashed half off its sliding rail and had closed with such force it was stuck in place. Garrick knelt, his knees creaking, and pointed. There was a dark stain down the door and across the deck, different in hue from the damp wood and the charcoal black from the fire.

"Blood?"

Fanta nodded, although from a casual glance it was difficult to be certain. Garrick fished in his pocket for a tissue to avoid leaving his own fingerprints on the handle as he heaved the cabin door open. It scraped across the rail, but remained open despite the tilted deck.

He was immediately struck by a pungent decaying smell from within that made him gag. He quickly swapped the tissue from the door to cover his nose and mouth. With the windows covered in grime, little light seeped in.

"Christ," he muttered.

Fanta was a little more resilient to the stench. She leaned over him, switching on her phone's torch and panning the light back and forth inside the cramped cabin. Garrick had been expecting to see the remains of a corpse, but instead he was greeted by clutter. The impact from beaching had caused the radio to jolt off the dashboard and smash onto the floor, its electronic guts spewing out. There was a large red plastic box lying on its side with the lid open, the contents of which were a mystery. Although as he took the light from Fanta's hand and got very close, he could see it was somewhat responsible for the smell.

At first, he assumed it was the remains of a dead gull trapped inside, but with Fanta's light they could see it was a fist-sized mass of gelatinous, unidentifiable flesh that a swarm of flies had gathered on. Now he became aware of the flies buzzing everywhere and swatted them away. His gag reflex kicked in, which was unusual for him as he was used to horrific crime scenes. He wondered if it was because this was unidentifiable and not at all human-like, or was he just becoming too old.

"That looks like somebody's lunch," Fanta muttered, her nose scrunching.

It took a moment for Garrick's mind to readjust to what she said, but then he saw it. It could well be the remains of somebody's as-yet-uncooked barbecue. He felt a wave of embarrassment regarding how he'd ` reacted, but the flies and the stench assured him he hadn't overreacted too much. He pulled himself out of the cabin and was thankful to take a deep breath of salty air to revive him.

They called in the discovery of the boat, and it was close to an hour before an officer from the East Sussex Constabulary turned up to stay at the site. The young woman seemed rather happy to spend her time hanging around on the beach. Garrick still wasn't sure what significance this discovery had. Abandoned for several days on a windy, rain-swept beach didn't give him much confidence they would find any usable evidence. But with the site secured and a forensic team unable to attend for at least six hours, he and Fanta took to canvassing the area for any additional clues. That was a thankless task, as for half a mile in every direction there was nothing but fields. The few houses that lined the main road had impressively high hedges, so any doorbell security cameras didn't have a view of the road.

Three miles away there was a petrol station and just beyond that a pub, both of which did have security cameras that Fanta put in a request to view. It was while waiting for her in the car that Garrick received an alarming text message from Wendy. She was experiencing pain in her belly and was calling an ambulance.

His first reaction was a sudden sickly feeling in the pit of his stomach. He tried to ring Wendy twice from the forecourt, ignoring the evil eye the woman at the petrol counter shot him for using his mobile. Both times he got straight through to her voicemail. He summoned every calming technique he could recall from his yoga classes. There was nothing he could do other than surf the time out until he made contact or reached the hospital. Panic would only interfere.

Garrick felt multitasking was something that came easy to him, but now, as they drove back to Kent with Fanta rabbiting on about the timescales in retrieving the footage from the Esso station, he couldn't quite focus on her words, and his thoughts went back to Wendy, pregnant with their child and suddenly on her way to hospital.

Fanta's Google Maps showed several other potential places to canvas, but Garrick was too eager to head home and mumbled that they should leave it to local police to scope out their home turf. He ignored Fanta's offer to drive them back and instead took the wheel himself, driving with such forcefulness that his DC remained silent and rigid.

Halfway through the journey he received another text from Wendy and swerved the car in his eagerness to read it, forcing Fanta to grab the wheel and bark a sharp reprimand at her boss. The message was scant on details and reassurance. All it said was she was at the maternity wing of the hospital. He called again, and it went to voicemail. Garrick's mouth was dry, so in answer to Fanta's concerned question about what was wrong, he simply tossed her his phone. She read the text and just nodded.

"She has to be careful," she said. "But I wouldn't worry too much. These things happen. Any slight pain, anything feeling wrong and," she made a whooshing sound, "straight off to A&E. Overkill, but sensible."

Garrick glanced at her. "And you'd know this how?"

"I'm a woman, guv," Fanta snapped back. "I know you think I'm a bit of a kid, but my sister was pregnant once."

"You have a sister?" Garrick ejected with surprise. "How big is your family?"

"Well..." Fanta trailed off. "Half-sister. Dad's side," she clarified. "Bear in mind, he's the one who named me Fanta, because he saw the drink can." She shot Garrick a challenging look. "His English didn't improve enough to get a job, so he eventually headed back to Hong Kong. 'Course, my parents split up by that point, and he had a family out there."

"Oh," Garrick trailed off, unsure whether he should be sympathetic or not.

"Anyway," Fanta cleared her throat. "I do have some valid points to say on this topic. And my valid point is: don't worry. The odds are that everything's fine."

To his incredible surprise, Garrick felt some solace from her words, although not quite enough to relent on his furious driving pace. When they reached Canterbury Hospital's car park, he left Fanta to deal with the car and he sprinted inside, only to be efficiently shepherded to a ward by a smiling nurse.

Anxious minutes passed before he was escorted to a ward. Wendy was asleep in the bed and just looking at her, Garrick suddenly felt an overwhelming exhaustion and a desire to hold her. He brushed a hand gently across her forehead and she awoke with a brief look of mild confusion which turned into a smile when she saw Garrick looming over her.

"What are you doing here?" she asked with a small smile.

"You scared the shit out of me."

Wendy pulled herself upright and gave a little snort of amusement. "I told you not to worry."

Garrick looked at her blankly. She never said anything like that. "I've been absolutely—"

He sucked in a breath, realising he was being pulled into a pointless argument. "What happened?"

"Oh God, I felt really bad cramps." Wendy ran her hand across her swollen abdomen. "I started to get worried. At one point it really hurt, I could barely stand. And..."

"And?" Garrick pressed.

"The ambulance came out surprisingly quickly." She smiled. "I thought the NHS was in crisis. They've been brilliant. They brought me here. They wanted to keep me in overnight but said there was nothing to worry about. Ultrasound and blood tests showed that baby is fine. We really need to agree on a name."

The name was one of those topics they had addressed early on, but since the chaos with his sister, it had never been raised since.

"She's fine? You're both fine?"

"Yep. Well, I'm in pain, but that's my job, isn't it? I'm the one in pain, you're the one who is a panicking pain." She grinned at him. "Relax. They said it's just one of those things. Muscle contractions, stress...." She shook her head. "My first child. Anything could happen. My body's not used to it."

Garrick experienced two simultaneous and conflicting feelings. The first was utter relief there was nothing wrong with Wendy and their baby. The second was the phrase "*first child*". For some reason, that frightened him. He was questioning whether he would be a good enough father for any child, never mind a *first* one.

He tried to let that slide, but for some reason it rattled around his head as Wendy continued giving him details of her time in the hospital. It also tempered his relief that she was okay. Satisfied she was going to be in for the night, and all was well, he kissed her goodbye and joined Fanta, who was waiting in the car, fielding phone calls and messages.

"We're not going to get anything from the ship until tomorrow," she told her boss. "What do you want to do now?"

"Go home, if that's alright with you, Fanta."

Chapter Seven

David Garrick sat alone in his small house, which felt empty without Wendy's presence flowing through every room. She was only staying in hospital for the night, but despite exhaustion making every movement a chore, Garrick couldn't sleep. He had regarded the house as a temporary reprieve from his own home before he sold it. It quickly turned into a loving, cosy refuge, and now as he stood in the half-finished baby's room, it was about to become a home. But not necessarily a home he could love. He'd sold his own homestead and was currently sitting on the money, debating what they should do in the future as a family. That very idea gave rise to yet more anxiety, so he shunted it away for future consideration.

The following morning, Wendy came home, all smiles, although from her movements, she was braving some discomfort, but she refused to mention it. David was so wrapped up in making sure she was comfortable and thinking about life in general that he didn't give the boat much more thought.

And with no other action needed on the case, he took the day off.

It was Chib who called him up two days later when he was in his local ASDA supermarket, wandering the aisles like a zombie. He caught himself using that rare moment of peace to relax and focus on himself.

"They were human remains, guv," Chib said bluntly. She was calling from the forensic office in East Sussex.

Garrick frowned as he recalled the scene on the boat. "I don't quite follow, Chib," he said.

"In the box. More specifically, the lab said it was human tissue. They can't match it exactly yet."

Garrick nodded hopefully before remembering he was on the phone and Chib couldn't see him. He cleared his throat. "Right, okay. Um... Could it be the remains of a fight?"

"The lab are conducting further tests. However, they did find traces of the victim's DNA on the boat."

Garrick felt the surge of adrenaline, a once-familiar jolt that he used to experience during breakthroughs in cases. Recently, he lamented how rare that feeling had become, as he had taken each increasingly worse crime within his stride. There had never been time to celebrate the victories.

He recalled a conversation he'd had during his young career with the senior officer who had shown him the ropes. He'd been warned to look out for signs that malaise was creeping in. It was the canary in the cage for police detectives. It was important not to become emotionally entangled with a victim's life, but empathy was still vital. When the empathy between a victim and an officer was gone, it was time to start considering a new career.

"I'm starting to feel excited again, Chib," he warned her.

"Our Jane Doe was on the boat. Can we get a fix on what happened?"

"There was evidence all over, in both the cabin and towards the back of the engines," said Chib, groping for the correct terminology.

"The aft," muttered Garrick.

"It suggests she was involved in a struggle. Blood specks from two other people were discovered on the cabin door and the engine throttle, although that was partially burned. The same for a baseball bat found on deck. It was charred, but there were traces of her blood on it. Dr Spackman confirmed the diameter of the base is consistent with the wounds on her neck."

"She was struck from behind."

"Then presumably tossed overboard shortly afterwards."

"It sounds more and more like a kidnapping to me," Chib said. "Who the heck is she?"

"I'm keeping the smuggling angle open, too. There is something not right about this whole thing."

"Sean is chasing the Coastguard and French authorities to see if we can get any match on the boat. But I wouldn't hold my breath on that. And as for smuggling, they searched for traces of gunpowder and narcotics. Nothing."

They were the two most indelible substances, traces of which were almost impossible to remove from a crime scene. Garrick tried to put himself into the victim's shoes. She'd been forced onto the boat. She'd struggled mid-journey and fallen, or been pushed, overboard after being struck across the head. There was organic matter on the boat, and she sported a recent operation wound. It didn't make any sense.

"What about the transponder?"

"Ah, we have Jane Doe's fingerprints on the switch. She was the last one to operate it."

"She turned it on. Why do that if you didn't want your position to be known. It was a call for help." He felt a taste of guilt, despite the fact there was no way he could have known about it. Despite all the advanced trafficking hardware on both sides of the Channel, there was nothing anybody could have done to save her life. "Maybe she started the fire on the engine too, as a distraction."

"Maybe." Chib's tone made it clear this was pure speculation and with no eyewitnesses, the truth would never be known.

Garrick pulled himself together and quickly wound up the call before completing the shopping at breakneck speed. He dropped the groceries back home but didn't even have time to unpack them before he had an exciting phone call from Fanta.

"Guv, I've got something!"

There was no mistaking the tangible atmosphere when David Garrick entered the incident room in Maidstone. He found his thoughts muddled and unfocused, which alarmed him. His doctor had placed him on a new set of medication before he returned to work, and he was beginning to think he was experiencing side effects. He parked in the station's secured car park, and scrambled to find his ID card to access the building. He first thought he'd left it at home, but then found it had slipped from his wallet somehow into the footwell of his car. He would definitely book an appointment with Dr Rajasekar to review his meds.

Only Fanta and DC Lord were in, and he headed

straight for the sparse-looking murder wall. It now had pictures of the boat, Jane Doe, and various maps, timecodes, and a printout of the ship's tracking data.

Lord gave a friendly nod, but was on the phone. Fanta was at her desk, absorbed with whatever was playing on her headphones. Garrick was about to make himself known but noticed she was filling out an application form for an inter-departmental promotion. The urge to interrupt was strong, but he resisted. It would be churlish to interfere, even if it would be self-destructive to encourage her too much. The unusual conflict of emotions tasted bitter, and he was thankful to see Chib enter with a cheery "Good morning" before suddenly remembering to ask about Wendy.

"She's fine, I think," Garrick replied. "She came home as if nothing had happened. Her stupid texts almost gave me a heart attack. But I'm told this is the stress of expecting a baby." He felt his cheeks flush when Chib threw him a sarcastic glance.

"Oh, you poor thing," she said.

"You know I didn't mean it that way," he said hesitantly. "I know I've got the easy end of the job, don't get me wrong. But stress is stressful."

Chib gave a non-committal grunt and sat at her desk. Harry hung up the phone. He had been half-listening and rolled his eyes.

"Don't let her give you a hard time, Guv. She's stressed over her passport."

"You would be too, if you knew how much the trip was costing. Why are they so damned slow?"

Keen not to push anybody's self-pity any further, Garrick threw his jacket over the back of his seat. Fanta looked up to acknowledge him, but held up a finger to indicate she wasn't ready to talk yet. Garrick joined Harry Lord in the small kitchen area across the corridor where his DC had made a swift escape. He was leaning against the counter, thoughtfully scrolling through his phone as a kettle boiled.

"Making the rounds again?" Garrick nodded to the coffee.

Harry slipped his phone away and took another cup. "Matcha tea?"

Garrick nodded thankfully. Harry's muted response added to the unusual atmosphere that was smothering the office today. Garrick was a natural observer, so he silently watched as Harry made the drinks and occasionally rubbed his leg. He had sustained a permanent injury after being struck by a car while on an investigation with Garrick. He now walked with a permanent limp, which others had accused him of playing up, although as time passed, it was increasingly obvious he wasn't. The pain also tended to be affected by the weather and the previous day's exercise regime. It was turning him into some poor, old, arthritic, rheumatoid sufferer.

Harry was always the first with inane, jovial banter, lightening the mood, tossing around casual insults, and generally bringing a thriving energy to a stressful environment. All of which was noticeably lacking today. It was clear he wasn't going to engage in conversation about it.

Garrick thought of a tactful way to spark the conversation. "What's the matter, Harry? You look like shit." Garrick remembered that he often wasn't the most tactful person. At least it triggered the ghost of a smile from his friend.

"I'm just thinking... about things. Y'know, life?"

Garrick nodded. "Living has crossed my mind every now and again."

Siren's Call

Harry rubbed his leg. "And this bastard is really getting to me. I feel office bound. If that makes sense."

As his superior officer, Garrick had never prevented Harry from taking part in any physical aspect of investigations. He had done so a couple of times, but his injury had always slowed him down. Garrick had tended to lean on Fanta who, as an ambitious young woman, constantly seizing any opportunity to prove herself.

"I know it's not great, but maybe... if you want to get out and follow leads..."

Harry pulled a face. "And slow everybody down? Unless you let me use my drone for work?" While Garrick was off, Harry had gotten into flying drones as a hobby. The others had warned him that Harry bored the ears off anybody he could corner to talk about it, so Garrick had actively avoided the topic.

"We need that Harry Lord skillset running the show around here."

Harry threw him a doubtful look and lifted the kettle as it came to the boil. He deliberately poured the water into an instant cup of coffee and then into the Matcha tea.

"Starbucks, here I come. Maybe policing has run its course for me."

"Don't tell me you're thinking of promoting yourself above the likes of me." Garrick forced a chuckle, but it sounded hollow and fake.

"Oh, you mean Fanta? Yeah, I know. Let's face it. She's going places."

"That's not what I meant," Harry said. "I meant being a copper in general. Perhaps there's another career awaiting my awesome skills." He handed Garrick the tea with the bag still in it.

"You're talking about private security. Jeez, it's the graveyard for ex-coppers. There's no way I could imagine you as a jaded security guard at Tesco. You'd hate it."

Fanta chose that moment to appear. She immediately picked up on the frosty atmosphere.

"What's going on here? Wait... I don't want to know."

"Drink?" Harry lifted the kettle.

"Some of us are busy, mate. I've received an ID on the organic matter found on the boat!"

Garrick's eyebrows raised quizzically when she didn't continue. "And?"

"Well... it's hard to explain. It might be easier if we check it out."

Chapter Eight

Fanta had dug up an address for a small council estate in Gravesend, the sort used by councils to dump any excess of population into cheap housing. It was almost a stereotypical impulse to say this was a crime hotspot. Statistically, that's exactly what it was. Garrick marvelled at the sheer audacity of cramming desperate people into an even more desperate environment.

Fanta had remained silent on what had specifically led her here, and instead they talked about Chib's pending honeymoon in the Maldives, and how if she didn't receive her passport in time, Fanta had volunteered to go. As she described the tropical paradise, Garrick realised that such a luxury was beyond him, especially with a child on the way. If he and Wendy did get married, perhaps the best they could look forward to was a static caravan in North Wales. It was reminiscent of his own childhood. The sheer thought of which sent a ripple of apprehension down his spine as the spectre of his now deceased sister rose in his mind; a person he had fought hard to expunge from his memory.

Now the indirect association drew a dreary spectre over his thoughts and gave him trouble focusing on the conversation.

Half the journey passed without him registering anything at all, and they were soon parking several doors from the address, in a narrow-terraced street, next to a waste bin that was overflowing and surrounded by black, uncollected bin bags.

Fanta exited the car, and Garrick immediately took in the range of multicultural faces slinking up and down the street, immersed in bubbles of their own business. Fanta consulted her phone and indicated several doors down.

"Ok, down here. Uroš Božović. A Serbian national."

"An illegal immigrant?"

Fanta shook her head. "No, not at all. He came over as a student studying engineering and architecture. He completed his bachelors last year. He was recently granted the right to stay, all perfectly legit. But that pound of flesh you found in the ship's cabin matches *him*."

"You found a DNA match?"

"From medical records at Maidstone."

Garrick followed Fanta to the dark green door that comprised mostly of flaking paint chunks. She knocked firmly on the door and waited, then followed up by pushing the bell twice. Garrick could clearly hear it ring from within the thin council-built walls. Receiving no answer, Garrick cupped his hands over the netted window and peered into the hallway that looked immediately out on the street, but he couldn't see any signs of activity. Fanta knocked again.

The door to the house on the right opened, and an old woman emerged, her head wrapped in a scarf framing a face pruned by a lifetime of hardship. She stood with an upright shopping trolley and looked at the two detectives with deep suspicion.

"He's not in," she said with a distinct Eastern European drawl.

"Do you know where he went?" asked Garrick.

The woman shook her head. "Haven't seen him for a week."

"Did he give you any indication of where he may be going?"

The woman's eyes narrowed. She shook her head. *"He's good lad."* It was the only information she offered before scurrying away down the street.

Garrick took a deep sigh. "Wonderful. So, we can either sit out here like morons or... get the place opened up." He peered through the letterbox and shouted, "Mr Božović! Police! We're hoping we could have a word."

He cocked his ear to the open flap but heard nothing. With another deep sigh, he looked at Fanta, but before he could speak, she was already on the phone ordering a locksmith to get them inside.

"You are becoming scarily efficient, DC Liu."

It only took 30 minutes for the locksmith to arrive.

"Are you on speed dial? Or is this another of your family members?" Garrick looked askance at Fanta.

"Always busy around here," said the locksmith, unfolding a pouch of tools. "Most people don't have a problem getting into places. It's patching them up where the dosh is."

He had the door open in less than a minute as he rammed a flexible plastic slide between the Yale lock's catch and the doorframe. It opened mere inches before a chain restricted it further. A pair of long-handled bolt cutters made short work of that.

Garrick and Fanta entered. The house was a small, cramped post-war build typical of most terraces, but it was well kept, broadcasting a sense of pride from the occupant. On the hall walls were photographs of Uroš. He was dark-haired, firmly built, and quite handsome. Most pictures were selfies of hiking around the countryside on his own. One proudly placed photograph showed him holding his diploma in engineering from Kent University. There were no signs of anything amiss in the flat, but it was clear he hadn't been here recently.

The living room was equally well presented. They moved into the kitchen and Fanta made straight for the refrigerator. She checked a plastic carton of milk and a packet of ham.

"From the use-by dates, he's been gone since last week."

They returned to the living room. Garrick read the spines of books on the shelf. They were mostly about engineering and architecture for healthcare with names he was unfamiliar with.

"Okay," Garrick said, glancing around with his hands extended. "Uroš left his home and, to all intents and purposes, is missing, until a blob of flesh turns up on a boat on its way back from France. On which, our Jane Doe was murdered. What does this tell us?"

"He's a clever, hygienic, legal citizen," Fanta said slowly as she processed the facts. "Recently qualified for work in a lucrative field. But he has to live in an area like this. So he doesn't have money. The flesh was sizeable. Forensics say it would be a life-threatening injury."

"So he's likely dead. Did our Jane Doe kill him? Did he attack her?"

"Or were they both victims?"

Silence filled the room. Broken suddenly by a ping from Fanta's phone. Her eyes widened as she read it.

"Holy socks. They have identified what part of Uroš it was." She met Garrick's gaze, as if not quite believing it. "It was a liver."

"Our Jane Doe had a new one..."

"They're comparing it now."

Garrick looked around the room with fresh eyes. "The guy is broke. She needs a new kidney. Did she buy it from him?"

"Buy it? You can't just pop it out. You'd die."

"No. You can donate one of your kidneys and still have an active healthy life. It's just that your days of drunken partying are over." He picked up Uroš's graduation photograph. "University isn't cheap. Maybe he owed the wrong people some money?"

With no further answers forthcoming from the property, Garrick and Fanta called DC Wilkes and instructed him to dig into Uroš's financial and work status so they could build a better picture of what he might have been doing on the boat.

They waited for the locksmith to make sure the door was secure behind them as they left. They returned to their vehicle with the intention of calling it a day and heading home, when Fanta received a message from Chib. She held up her phone so Garrick could read.

"Next stop, Maidstone Hospital!"

Chib was waiting for them in the car park of Maidstone Hospital. She'd spent the time sitting in her car, poring over her phone. She was so distracted that she jumped when Garrick rapped on the side door window.

"Evening, Detective Sergeant," Garrick said, easing the phrase out in a humorously long way. "I was thinking I was heading home for a spot of DIY. And you dragged me back into civilisation, away from the perils of IKEA."

He felt slightly uneasy when it took Chib a few seconds to reciprocate. His team were normally more on the ball with his creaky humour, and he feared that he was being relegated, quite literally, into the Dad Zone of tedious, inappropriate humour.

Chib put her phone away and climbed from her car. "Uroš had been here recently."

"How recent?"

"Two weeks. The 17th, to be precise."

"OK," Garrick noted. "What for?"

Chib hesitated, uncertain how to continue. "Well... I think it's best we all talk to the person who remembers the situation."

With this left hanging cryptically in the air, she led the way in, past the receptionist at the desk, giving her a courteous nod, alleviating the need to flash any warrant cards. Garrick had been expecting to follow her through to a ward, but instead, Chib took a less trodden path into a narrow corridor. Through a secure door which she opened with a temporary access card she'd been given, and then down some steps into the basement.

They walked briskly through more functional corridors, through the operational bowels of the hospital itself. They reached a plain door marked 206. She gave a quick knock, then entered without waiting for an invitation. Garrick and Fanta exchanged a curious look before following.

Room 206 was lit by an ailing fluorescent light that cast shadows amongst the basic steel shelving and racks of computer servers. In the corner was a chipped wooden desk, on which a computer was splayed open, its innards exposed, and a graphics card had been removed waiting for a replacement. The table around it was covered in tools, screws, and an empty metal curry tray that was half-stuffed in a paper bag, casting Asian aromas and making Garrick's stomach rumble.

"This is Wayne." Chib gestured to a young black man with short dreads pulled stylishly back. He stood next to a server, clipping network cables back in place. He offered a friendly smile and a nod.

"Alright."

"Hi, Wayne," Garrick offered his hand, which the man quickly shook, and then did the same to Fanta.

"You're real detectives, eh?" he said, looking between the three of them. He nodded at Garrick. "You fit the bill."

Fanta burst into laughter. "You don't get more diverse than us."

Chib smiled. "Oh yeah, it's like a bad joke. An Asian, a black woman, and a pasty-faced white guy walk into a bar..."

Garrick looked slightly perplexed and found himself smiling like an idiot.

"I believe you have something useful regarding our case," Garrick pulled himself together. "My DS here was vague, to the point of annoyance."

"Oh yeah, yeah," Wayne nodded. "She was asking about that incident two weeks ago. It was weird, but I'm not sure if it's relevant." Wayne tapped his seat. "So, I'm IT, as you've probably figured out. Which most of the time means I sit here, get the odd call out, and I try to fix stuff." He pointed to himself. "The unsung hero of the NHS, right here." He sat down. "Now, there's four of us on a rota, including night shifts. I was just about at the end of transitioning off my day shift, looking forward to heading out to the pub, when I get a call. Usual bad timing."

He leaned back in his chair. "Most of the time, it's small stuff. Computers crashing, people forgetting passwords, all that sort of stuff. We used to get to do everything, but cutbacks, contracts being tendered out, you know, anything that can't be quickly fixed has to go out to an external company. And of course we don't touch any of the medical equipment, that's way out of my pay grade."

Wayne opened his laptop. "They call, complaining there's a problem with the database. Now, I don't get to touch the database. There's a lot of patient confidentiality software," he waved his hand dismissively. "Not my job unless it's a password problem. But the nurse in question was not having a good day, and I feel sorry for him. So, I just took a look on my way out in case it was the computer glitching."

He glanced at Chib. "Now, you said you don't need a warrant for any of this? I don't wanna get in trouble."

Chib shot Garrick a guilty look and shook her head. "You can willingly show us whatever you need. It's absolutely fine." She caught Fanta's amused expression.

Wayne nodded and indicated his laptop. "Just be clear, this isn't the database itself. These are just screenshots I had to take for diagnostics. So, nurse has a patient who comes in, suffering some internal bleeding. They match the records to this bloke."

Garrick leaned in, and then with an uncomfortable glance at the younger officers, he squinted so he could read the file. He swore his vision was far worse than it was last month. He should really add a trip to Specsavers to his to-do list.

Siren's Call

"Uroš," he said. He glanced at Chib, who nodded enthusiastically.

"He came in with a bleeding injury. A wound had opened," Wayne explained.

Garrick nodded. "I don't see what the issue is. Is some information missing?"

Wayne sniggered. "You could say that. Not so much missing, as this Uroš guy had a bigger problem than an open wound. He was a *woman*."

"A woman?" exclaimed Fanta. "You mean, transgender?"

Wayne shook his head and chuckled, "No, I mean a totally fit bird." He suddenly became self-conscious. "Well, I mean, no offence, it's an attractive woman who looked very much..." He trailed off. "She was definitely female," he concluded in a sober voice.

"So the records must be wrong. Must be. Somebody screwed up somewhere, something's been badly assigned. But it's a bit of a serious bleed out she had, but the woman wasn't giving anything away. She didn't want to give a name, didn't want to give a National Insurance number, nothing. She was looking for somebody, but she wouldn't say who. It was crazy. I thought she was on drugs or something."

"What did she look like?"

"Yeah, about 5'6". Kind of half Indian, but a pale complexion. Really pretty. Deep brown eyes, a bit of French accent. Like I said, she was quite attractive," Wayne added, drifting off again.

Chib held up her phone. "Did she look like this?"

Wayne gave her a knowing look. "That's the woman you showed me before. That's her."

Chib angled the phone around so the others could see

their Jane Doe. The bricks of conspiracy were clattering into place.

"The nursing staff stemmed the bleeding. Shot her full of drugs and when they came back, she'd gone. Scarpered out of the hospital. Obviously didn't want any questions asked." He shrugged. "Now we get all kinds of weird in here, all the time, so I didn't make too much of it. The only reason it stuck with me so much is because I had to stay behind for an extra three hours waiting for the database contractor and checking there was no hardware glitch on our end."

"What caused the bleeding?"

Wayne shrugged. "A scar had opened up on her back." He indicated the same place Jane Doe had her scar. "It was about here. Seeped through her clothes. It looked pretty sick. Red and inflamed. She was in a lot of pain."

Finally, Garrick felt as if they were on the trail of the phantom woman. Was she the victim? Or was that the new Serbian addition to the puzzle? He was sure the security footage would soon hand them a victory.

Chapter Nine

The following day, Garrick was reviewing the collection of security footage from the hospital. A task Fanta would have ordinarily jumped at. He was surprised to find that she had taken a rare day of leave, which was very unlike her, especially considering how hands-on she had been during the investigation.

Harry Lord thought she was attending a job interview, although he was a little vague on the facts. Which, again, was very unlike Harry. Garrick wondered if he was being deliberately ambiguous to cover for his colleague. An admirable, but irritating character trait.

With accurate time stamps, it took minutes to finally see the face. There was absolutely no doubt that this was Jane Doe. Wayne had relayed his side of the story with admirable accuracy. Switching through files as Jane Doe moved through the hospital, they were able to track her progress back into the car park, shortly after a nurse had applied new stitches and dressed the wound. The woman was frail, barely able to stand without swaying, yet she had no intention of hanging around the hospital. Chib, Sean, and Harry all watched as she staggered into a wall, pausing only for a moment to catch her breath before pressing on.

"I see what he meant about being drugged," said Chib.

"She's like the Terminator," Harry muttered.

"She's bleeding and in pain. What would prevent her from staying in the hospital?"

"She's being chased," said Sean Wilkes. "Worried the law would find her."

Harry shook his head. "Can't be. She's not wanted for anything. We're struggling to identify her, and we have her body on a slab!"

"Then she's worried about being identified in the hospital," Chib suggested reluctantly. "But I showed the picture around, and asked admin to make sure all staff saw it. Nobody has come forward."

Garrick snapped his fingers. "But she was looking for somebody. Another patient? Or an employee?"

Sean switched to footage from another security camera as they tracked her progress into the car park, where she headed towards a white Range Rover."

"Can we get a plate?" said Garrick, squinting again.

"Not from this angle. And the car park doesn't have ANPR," Chib said with a sigh. Automatic Number Plate Recognition was a lifesaver in most cases. The public generally hated it, as it was synonymous with speed cameras and, in some cases, accusations regarding invasion of privacy. But when it came to tracking criminals down, the good far outweighed the bad.

Twenty seconds after Jane Doe exited, a man dashed from the hospital in pursuit. The two had a heated conversation at her car, before she got in and drove away. They followed the man's progress as far as they could, as he left the hospital grounds.

"Who the hell was that guy?" said Garrick.

They had two clear images of his face and Garrick circulated them back to the hospital to see if they knew who he was. Twenty minutes later he received an email confirming the name: Dr Kabir Iyer, a consultant surgeon who was sometimes based at the hospital. Garrick studied the image. He estimated the doctor to be on the small side, maybe 5 foot 5, slightly overweight, at least in his mid-fifties with a short crown of hair around his spreading bald patch, and round spectacles with thick black frames. His name suggested Indian descent.

It was just after lunch that very same day that he and Chib drove in her near-silent Nissan Leaf electric car to Dr Iyer's home address, out in the rolling hills of the picturesque North Downs.

Chib gave a low whistle as they cut through acres of farmers' fields and woodland, with occasional rolling views of the Garden of England teased before them. Each house they passed stood away from the road, accessed by a large driveway. There was only ever a glimpse of an impressive building beyond the meticulously tended trees.

"Quite a nice place to live," she said. Being a London girl and living in Orpington, Chib never had the chance to explore the countryside on her doorstep.

Garrick nodded, noting some of the houses' garages were bigger than the house he rented with Wendy.

"A lot of celeb types out here. Musicians, TV presenters, comedians, and a bunch of crooks." He shot Chib a thin smile. "They're not *necessarily* one and the same."

"He must be earning quite a bit to be able to afford a place like these."

Garrick leafed through a small file Harry had managed to put together. Garrick had insisted he print it out, rather than stare at the small screen on his phone. Dr Kabir Iyer was a dual British-Indian citizen who had practised in the swanky Harley Street in London before being hit by a malpractice suit. Although it seemingly had no merit, it had disrupted his life enough to make him start fresh outside of London. His name had come up on several private medical sites. Outsourcing their skills to the private sector was a lucrative additional revenue stream for any NHS practitioner.

Although he couldn't deny he was jealous of the man's success, Garrick couldn't blame him. Since coming back from America, at the back of his mind, he had even been entertaining ideas of quitting the police force and starting his own private detective agency, with thoughts of Sam Spade and Philip Marlowe flitting through his imagination. But it was just his imagination. He knew the life of a private detective, especially in the UK, was one primarily of chasing cheating spouses and lost pets. It was very far from a romantic get-rich-quick scheme portrayed in the movies.

"Here we go," said Chib as she flipped the indicator, following the instructions on her satnav. "This is Iyer's pile right here."

The gate was closed. Chib buzzed the intercom but received no answer. Garrick stepped out of the vehicle and discovered the gate was not locked, merely pulled closed. He swung it open for Chib to enter and followed her up the short gravel driveway to a large, converted barn that looked like something from the TV show *Grand Designs*. Sunlight gleamed from panoramic windows and immaculate tiles, giving the impression the structure had *just* been completed. There was an obligatory red Porsche Carrera in the driveway.

Chib parked and joined him. "Nice for some, isn't it?" he said with resignation.

Chib elbowed him in the arm. "Cheer up, Guv. Don't let it get you down. If it makes you feel any better, you can think of me in the Maldives next week."

"It may surprise you, but that is not as comforting a thought as you might think it is."

Chib tutted. "When I get back you can take great satisfaction that I'll be paying for it for the next decade."

Garrick grinned. "You're right, that does make me feel better."

As they approached the house, they noticed several security cameras poised around the property. Nobody answered the doorbell, and Garrick was about to circle round into the backyard when he noticed the folding door to the separate large double-garage wasn't quite closed. There was a half-foot gap above the floor.

The two detectives strolled closer. Garrick slid on a pair of blue latex gloves that were rolled in his Barbour's pocket and gripped the underside of the garage door. His knees clicked as he crouched and, remembering to lift with his knees so he didn't put his back out, he heaved it upward.

His nostrils were immediately assaulted by a familiar smell. Blood.

Clear plastic strips, the sort found in storage depots, stretched from floor to ceiling, veiling the entrance. Beyond them was darkness. Chib gently nudged between them, her phone raised, its flashlight on, illuminating the space beyond.

"Wow," her voice echoed as she stepped inside.

Garrick followed closely behind. His first instinct was that they'd walked onto a film set. Chib's light played off a polished steel table in the centre of the room, with a large parasol like medical light arcing over it. The floor and walls were clinical white panels, which even stretched overhead, forming a sealed box. Long white work surfaces lined one wall, fitted with a large surgical sink and a range of gleaming surgical knives, saws and other equipment that made Garrick shudder. To the side, stood a pair of large industrial-sized stainless-steel freezers.

Garrick found a light switch. Recessed LED lights cast the room with an almost blinding pure light.

"A DIY operating theatre," Chib muttered. "Now, that's something you don't see every day." She began recording a video to document the scene.

"I'm pretty sure most surgeons don't have these at home. I thought they were all into golf."

With everything neatly fitted, there was nowhere that a body could hide. Garrick approached the freezers, his eyes searching for signs of blood spatter. Everything had been scrubbed clean, and from the lingering scent of bleach, quite recently.

He took a deep breath and opened the nearest freezer. The blast of frigid air was a relief from the cloying humidity in the room. The shelves were empty, save a pair of small red, plastic thermal boxes, like the one they had found on the boat. Fighting his inherent revulsion, Garrick slowly took one out, drew one half out and prised open the lid, bracing himself to see something disgusting. It was empty and spotlessly clean. He pushed it back onto the shelf and closed the refrigeration doors in case any of the evidence would spoil.

He closed the door and opened the second unit. Inside

Siren's Call

were packs of blood that he could only assume were human, marked with various types: A, B, AB and O, marked with positive and negatives.

"Jesus," Garrick muttered under his breath. "He's prepared for everyone."

He looked at Chib but couldn't find any words to express what they'd found. He gave a gentle shake of the head in disbelief and motioned to quickly exit the garage, because he could now taste the bleach at the back of his throat.

Outside in the cool fresh air, he sucked in a deep breath and pulled the shutter back down.

"I'll call this in," said Chib.

Garrick nodded and continued around the property to a back gate. It was ajar. His eyes clocked a security camera that covered both the house and garage, and he braced himself for the possibility of an attack. He crept around to the side until he reached a kitchen door.

He drew in another deep breath, grasped the handle, levered it down and gave a gentle push. The door was unlocked. He entered a small, pristine utility room with polo-shirts, chinos, and underwear piled on the counter, ready to be washed. He pushed on through into the kitchen, which was beautifully appointed and spotless, looking as if it had leapt from the pages of a sales brochure.

"Kent Police!" he yelled. "We are entering the property. Please make yourself known." He strained to listen but was met with silence. He was so focused that he flinched at the sudden noise behind him as Chib entered. He pressed his hand over his heart. "Are you trying to kill me, Chib?"

"Not at the moment, guv," she said with a terse edge in her voice as her eyes flicked around. "This feels so wrong."

Garrick nodded. They stepped through a large archway

into a hall with a staircase to one side and two rooms branching off. He indicated to the left and they drew closer.

"Kent Police," he bellowed again. "If anybody's in the property, make yourself known."

They stepped into a large living room. The designer chic perfectly fitted within the rest of the house. A quick glance didn't reveal anything amiss. Garrick retraced his steps across the hallway and into the other room. He stopped so suddenly, Chib bumped into him.

"I think we've found him," he muttered darkly.

The room was a library, with shelves of books sporting esoteric medical titles in English and Hindi. A large wooden writing desk dominated the middle of the room, stacked with journals and medical books.

In the chair was Kabir Iyer. He was slumped backward. Somebody had slit him open from the gut, through his ribcage, up to his throat. The floor and desk were awash with congealed blood and his internal organs had cascaded out, spattering in a grisly mosaic across the floor. The only area on the desk that was clear of blood was an empty rectangle where Garrick guessed a laptop would have lain.

Both detectives were hardened veterans of crime scenes, but there was something so coarse and brutal about this one that made them both retch. Kabir Iyer's eyes were open, gazing to infinity, his mouth ajar, and his tongue a ragged slab of meat that had been sliced diagonally.

He looked at Chib. "Get everybody here," he said. "I have a feeling this case has mob connections."

Chapter Ten

The uniformed officers turned up within 20 minutes and set about guarding the entrance. Another two officers helped conduct a further search of the house and grounds.

Immediately upon finding the body of Kabir Iyer in the library, Garrick and Chib had continued searching the house. Downstairs there was another large lounge at the rear of the property and conservatory overlooking a spacious garden where nothing seemed to be amiss. It was upstairs in the bedroom that they found a second body that had been butchered on the bed. Chib's immediate and correct assumption was that it was the surgeon's wife, Vanessa.

She lay face up, fully clothed, her throat slit. Internal organs had been pulled out onto the blood-soaked duvet. The attack had been so savage that they couldn't spot a single surface that wasn't covered in blood, including streaks across the ceiling and the recessed lighting fixtures.

The initial forensics team arrived just over two hours later, led by Zoe, an Australian woman with dyed blue hair, cut in a bob. She beamed at Garrick as she entered the library.

"You're looking well, poppet. I haven't seen you since you buggered off on that American business. Heard about it though."

Garrick shrugged. "No one had the courtesy of being murdered since then."

"Looks like they've made up for it now, mate," she said, casting a professional eye around the library.

Unlike Garrick, there seemed to be nothing that fazed her. A consummate professional, he often wondered what it would take to throw Zoe off balance. He suspected that it was either the embrace of some fluffy kittens, or that beneath her charm lay some serious grit that enabled her to perform in places where even hardened soldiers would fear to tread. If not, she was a genuine sociopath.

"And I hear it's a double-wubble," she said, indicating upstairs. Garrick nodded. She pursed her lips suggestively. "The things you do to see me. It's adorable."

"You're worth it."

Zoe cocked her head curiously. "It's the other one splayed out like this?"

"Yes," said Chib, who had been watching Zoe's customary flirtations with amusement. "It feels very ceremonial. Like a warning sign."

Zoe circled round the corpse. "Yeah, that's what I was thinking. It puts me in mind of Jack the Ripper," she said. She leaned closer to the gaping wound across the ribcage. "It's a clean cut. Without obvious signs of hacking. Something like that requires a helluva lot of force."

A few questions flashed through Garrick's mind, but he remained silent as he listened to Zoe's chain of thought.

Siren's Call

"Reminds me, you had your kid yet?" she suddenly asked him.

"Um, no. Soon."

"Ah. Shame. Good ones are always nabbed early on." Zoe indicated the clear rectangle on the desk. "Take it you didn't move anything?"

Garrick shook his head. "I'm guessing it was a laptop."

Zoe's brow knitted together. "If you want me to make a guess, I'd say it's a 13-inch Apple MacBook."

Garrick was impressed. "What makes you say that?"

Zoe rolled her eyes. "Power pack still under the table, mate."

Garrick pulled himself together. He could feel that events were getting on top of him, and he felt a wave of fatigue wash over him. His immediate thought was of Wendy and how she was coping alone. It was enough of a reason for him to finally excuse himself from the crime scene and return home, leaving orders for him to be contacted when the forensic team was winding up its preliminary investigations.

Back home in his cramped house, the old moniker 'crime doesn't pay' rang in his ears. Kabir's palatial house was consistent not just with a successful surgeon, but with somebody who had lucrative dealings in crime. And like most of them, he had finally met his match.

Garrick found Wendy on the sofa, watching the TV quiz show, Pointless, surrounded by the remains of her lunchtime dishes. She beamed at Garrick as they exchanged a kiss before she wrinkled her nose and protested at how disgusting he smelled. He'd planned for a quick shower which transformed into an overly long bath before he returned downstairs to find Wendy snoozing in front of the local news.

He searched the kitchen for something to eat, but his stomach only navigated him towards a single packet of crisps. He was really feeling out of sorts. He cleared Wendy's dishes and sat next to her, half-watching the television and failing to get any answers right. She shifted position to nuzzle against him. His hand rested gently on her swollen stomach, and he was thrilled when he felt a tiny kick.

"We've got a footballer," he quipped.

Wendy smiled, but it was clear she'd heard that joke one time too often. Maybe it was time for him to take early retirement? Fanta was moving on; Harry was already thinking of early retirement and Chib wasn't shy about her ambitions to move up. Only Sean Wilkes seemed happy with his current lot in life. With each meaningless death, the value of life was becoming a more intrinsic question for him. His gaze cast to his fossil cleaning kit on the dining room table, which he'd noted had been pointedly pushed aside to the far end and covered with various baby gifts they'd received from friends and family.

With swirling thoughts of future plans, which were marred by the depressing knowledge murder victims no longer had a future, Garrick drifted into a fitful slumber. He woke to find Wendy had disappeared upstairs to bed. Glancing at his phone, he was glad he hadn't missed any calls.

He followed Wendy up the darkened staircase towards the bedroom door. For a second, a tremor of paranoia washed over him, as memories of previous horrors bubbled beneath his consciousness. His heart began to hammer in his chest.

He had rigorously attended all the therapy courses the force's HR department had offered him after events with his sister, yet still he felt the fragile membrane between the past and the present was occasionally shaken in the presence of death.

Pulling himself together, he stepped into the bedroom to see Wendy was sound asleep with a blindfold on. She had taken to wearing it after claiming the feeble light from Garrick's bedside lamp kept waking her. An impressive feat considering he could barely read a book by it. He dressed down into a clean pair of pyjama shorts and delicately climbed into bed. Wendy's gentle snoring was peaking every thirty seconds or so, robbing the opportunity for him to fall asleep. His mind began to race as he tried to explore what circumstances had led to the murder of Dr Iyer and his wife. Daylight peeked through the curtains before he eventually fell asleep. His last thoughts resigned to the fact that his planned restful evening at home had turned into a complete washout. His final thought was to schedule an appointment with his private physician, Dr Rajasekar, and ask for sleeping tablets to see him through for the next month.

It was his ringing phone followed by Fanta's overly perky voice that woke him with a start. It was just after eight in the morning, and she was telling him to make it back to Iyer's house as soon as possible. She almost barked it as an order, no doubt rehearsing for her future job.

Ordinarily, Garrick would have bolted through the door to attend the crime scene as fast as he could. Instead, he took time to have breakfast with Wendy. He ate some Crunchy Nut cereal with a splash of cold milk, then stole a piece of jam-slathered toast from Wendy's plate. All the while, he listened patiently to her narration about the antenatal class she'd attended the previous day, and the gossip circulating between the mothers-to-be. She was relieved that she was no longer in any pain, although her back was close to giving up. Garrick listened and made comforting noises when he could. It was more of a monologue than a conversation, but he was happy to sit there and listen to a life that sounded so normal and drama-free.

Her last words stayed with him as he drove to work. She was quoting her mother who stated that all the babies in her family had been born a few weeks premature. She was convinced this little tigress was going to be escaping very soon.

Returning to Kabir Iyer's house, Garrick was struck by the image of the circus coming to town. The entire driveway was filled with white forensic tents and police vehicles were parked along the country lane's grass verge. He was greeted by a beaming Fanta.

"Morning, Guv," she said perkily, handing him a cardboard cup of hot green tea.

Garrick looked at it suspiciously. Such generosity was very much out of character for the young DC. He looked around. "Where's Chib?"

Fanta shook her head. "She's spending time at the hospital doing face-to-face interviews with Wayne and the staff who'd worked with our doctor. He also worked privately for a number of clinics, so he had quite an extensive network of people. Sean's chasing them down."

Before he realised it, Garrick found himself following DC Liu towards the front door, which was blocked by a short forensic tent with a double plastic sheet strapped across the entrance to limit external contamination.

"You never told me how the interview went."

Fanta looked sheepish and gave a little shrug. "Who knows?" She gestured towards the garage. "That is definitely a state-of-the-art home theatre, and not the kind of place he's putting on a puppet show for kids."

"He was ready for anything. The only people who do that, that I can think of, are Mafia doctors."

"Cool! Like, pulling bullets out of injured hitmen, all off the record? That sort of thing?"

"Just like the movies."

Inside, the library was covered with small plastic cones and incident flags highlighting various pieces of evidence. There were no forensic officers in the room.

"So far, as Zoe and her team were able to ascertain, the good Doctor—"

"Mr," Garrick corrected her.

"Huh?"

"Surgeons are called misters, not doctors."

"Why?"

"I have no idea. It's one of those great mysteries of life."

"Anyway, Mr Dr Kabir Iyer was killed here at his desk. The body is at the pathologist's, but Zoe's guess was that it was a slow death. He was probably paralysed as there was little resistance as he was butchered on the spot."

Garrick circled round the desk, noting the little plastic numbered cone where the laptop had once been. He replayed the situation through his mind and indicated the chair.

"He was sitting here with his attacker at the laptop. If they were to kill him that quickly, perhaps they were standing behind him here." Garrick moved around and stood behind the chair. "That would mean they have a clear line of sight on this missing laptop. What does that indicate to you?"

Fanta paused as she thought it through. "That they needed files off it, or they at least needed him to unlock the laptop before doing him in."

"Exactly. The murder is premeditated. To be premeditated, there would have to be reason, so it wasn't a crime of passion. Was anything else taken?"

"Not that we can determine."

Garrick tapped his finger thoughtfully against his lips. "Something had gone wrong somewhere. And the likelihood is that any incriminating evidence would have been on that laptop."

"So, the obvious connection is our Jane Doe from the boat. She comes to see him in the hospital because she is injured. She has the operation here. And not in the hospital."

"That's pushing the notion of private health care to the extreme, but let's go with it."

"And then we have a two-week window when she's suddenly found dead on a beach returning from France."

They both lapsed into a moment's silence as they imagined the grisly assault taking place.

"It doesn't draw us any closer to the identification of our original victim," Garrick mused.

Fanta chewed her lip thoughtfully. "We never got the reg of the Range Rover she was driving at the hospital."

"Our mystery woman visits our mob doctor. A couple of weeks later, he ends up dead, and then so does his wife."

He followed Fanta's lead into the kitchen. There were a few more cones and the area leading to the utility room was blocked by police tape. Fanta pointed at the floor.

"So we have your size nines clomping through there, across valuable evidence." She mischievously caught Garrick's eye. "And there was another set of footprints that don't match any of the shoes in the house. Somebody tried to clean them." She gestured to a broom in the utility room. "But not enough to totally remove residue. Those tracks come in and out of the house. Forensics think they've identified the same imprint on the carpet upstairs."

"Just one set of tracks? One assailant."

Fanta nodded. "This does look like a one-man job so far. But here's the thing, the killer came in and attacked Mrs Iyer right here." She extended her arms around the kitchen. "Now, pending a coroner's report, the guess is she was knocked unconscious here and then dragged upstairs, where she was killed on the bed. Due to the lack of struggling, we think she was unconscious when she was... cut open." Fanta hesitated as the image of the corpse rose in her mind's eye. She pulled herself together and moved to the doorway so they had a clear view of the hall and the front door. "Now Kabir Iyer's footprints come straight from his car into the house and stop in the hallway here. Indications are this is where he was intercepted by the killer and then carted into the library."

"So what was the point in killing the wife?" Garrick asked.

"Maybe in case he tried to escape, or maybe if he wasn't intercepted here. Who knows?"

Garrick wasn't convinced. Even random attacks by psychopaths had their own internal logic, buried in the assailant's psyche, no matter how twisted and distorted it was. He moved back into the library and looked around the room. One shelf contained blood-splattered travel books from every corner of the planet. There was a large globe in the corner and a small magnetic map of the world hung on the wall, with little silver magnets highlighting various destinations that he guessed the surgeon had travelled to.

"The wife, it just doesn't ring true," Garrick mused. "Zoe said all of this reminded her of Jack the Ripper. His murders were arranged to convey a message. Like this. A message or a warning to somebody else. Killing the wife reinforces that message very clearly."

"A message to who?" Fanta asked.

"That is the specific question that needs addressing." He paused, then added, "A message to opponents."

"I don't get it," Fanta replied, looking blank.

"Think about it. The killer, whoever he works with, whether he was the boss... This is all orchestrated by somebody above Kabir Iyer. That means his services were for hire, and the doctor was either on their side and had screwed up, or he was on another side and was paying the price. Either way, I think this indicates there were two sides, and Kabir Iyer and his wife were totems in this war."

"That's a pretty brutal message," said Fanta.

"And this kind of brutality usually centres around the world of hard drugs. And I'm talking drugs with serious street value. Gangs run by people who are not known for their table manners. Kabir Iyer is a mob-doctor for hire, with his own surgery here. Something's gone wrong, and his screw-up is connected to our Jane Doe." Garrick paced the room, his mind working through the possibilities. "What we've got to do is figure out that connection."

"If she was a key operative in this organisation, maybe she'd been injured. Needed medical treatment but couldn't find Iyer. So, she went to the hospital. He later had to replace a damaged kidney. That goes wrong. The doctor pays the price for a botched operation."

The detectives knew that spinning a good yarn, based on the most tenuous of facts and speculation, was always good practice. Even wildly wrong theories could steer an investigation onto the right track.

"Nice. But she'd already had the surgery, remember?"

"Okay. But that doesn't mean the rest of it doesn't fit."

"True. But then why was she beaten on the boat?"

"The rival gang."

Garrick slowly nodded in agreement. "The rival gang to our phantom mob-boss."

They both fell silent as they contemplated the various scenarios, hoping something in the room would spring out and draw their attention to a vital clue.

Finally, Garrick spoke again. "We need to dig deeper into Kabir Iyer's background. His finances, his travel history, any connections to known criminals or drug traffickers. And we need to push harder on identifying our Jane Doe. She's the key to all this, I'm sure of it."

"I'll get on it," Fanta said, her earlier perkiness replaced by determination. "I'll have the team look into it all. And I'll check with Sean if there's any progress on identifying the woman from the boat."

Garrick nodded approvingly. "Good. And I want to take

another look at the crime scene upstairs. There might be something we've missed."

As they made their way up the stairs, Garrick couldn't shake the feeling that they were only scratching the surface of something much bigger. The brutality of the murders, the missing laptop, the mystery woman – it all pointed to a complex web of criminal activity. And somewhere in the middle of it all was Dr Kabir Iyer, the surgeon who seemed to have a foot in both the legitimate and criminal worlds. They had a long road ahead of them. But for now, all they could do was follow the evidence and hope it would lead them to the truth.

A sudden, victorious whoop from upstairs made them both run up the last few steps. Garrick led the way towards the sounds from the bedroom. Here they found two white-smocked forensic officers gathered around a wardrobe, one taking photographs.

"Having fun, lads?" said Garrick.

The forensic officer, who was half inside the wardrobe, peeked out and grinned. "We've got the safe open, guv."

Garrick nodded, although he hadn't had time to read any reports, so wasn't aware there was a safe in the building. "Excellent."

The forensic officer stood back as the second man moved in, taking rapid photos of the safe's contents. He backed away, allowing Garrick to peek inside. There was a mound of cash. Garrick could see it was all in crisp £20 and £50 notes.

"Bloody hell," he muttered. "What do you reckon? £100,000... £200,000?"

"I reckon that's clocking on to a quarter of a million at least, guv."

Once again, Garrick hated the fact crime paid so well. It

was a lot of loose change to have lying around the house, especially for a prominent, respected surgeon.

Fanta pointed to an object in the safe. "Odd place to keep his car keys."

Garrick frowned. He recalled seeing Kabir Iyer's Porsche keys on the hall table, where they'd remained undisturbed. He gestured for the forensic officer to fish them out. The officer laid them in his gloved hands so Garrick could make a closer inspection. There were two keys. One that looked like a regular Yale key, the other like a car key, with a chunky black fob with a silver logo he didn't recognise.

"Are there any other vehicles on the property?" Fanta shook her head. Garrick took a closer look at the logo on the fob. When he turned it around, it looked like a stylised letter P. "That's not a car brand I recognise. Anybody?"

Fanta and the forensic guys hadn't seen it before. Fanta used her phone to take a close-up photo of the logo. A few taps on the image and she smiled.

"Got it!" exclaimed Fanta triumphantly. She held up her phone displaying an internet search of the very same logo.

Garrick was impressed. "That was fast work, detective."

"I'm embracing the power of AI."

Garrick gave a blank look, once again feeling the world around him was outpacing his age. He felt a twinge of pride and annoyance that he was looking at Fanta, who was clearly the face of the future. When he found his voice, his mouth was a little dry. "Don't we all. So, what is it?"

"Pursuit. It's a boat manufacturer," said Fanta with a gleam in her eye. "It's an ignition key."

Chapter Eleven

On any case, it was essential that information was shared and regularly updated. While evidence and procedures were recorded on HOLMES, the force's computer system named after the fiction detective, there was no guarantee everybody was paying attention to every aspect. In addition, they were now working on the assumption that the Jane Doe and Dr Kabir Iyer cases were linked by the same killer, although they couldn't ignore the outside possibility that it was all a ghastly coincidence. But one thing Garrick had long since stopped believing in was coincidence.

Back in the station, he stood before the murder board. It still had plenty of space, which was an unhealthy testament to how little progress they had made. The pictures of all three victims now hung on the wall, with Uroš Božović pinned to the side, his whereabouts unknown. Harry Lord was conducting deep research into Vanessa Iyer, but so far had turned up nothing more than she enjoyed being a housewife and lapping up the luxuries her husband's status and salary provided.

Photos of the boat and the beach where it was found ran along the bottom, with various handwritten notes indicating the time it was found and references to the forensic search that had taken place on board. CCTV footage stills from the hospital were pinned centrally, showing the deceased woman and Kabir Iyer talking together in the hospital car park.

Garrick added a photograph of the boat ignition key, with a note about the brand. Fanta was at her desk, making calls and fielding queries to the boat manufacturer to try and get an ID on the actual model. That would give them somewhere to start looking.

DC Wilkes had started to extrapolate any strand they could from Kabir Iyer's hospital connections to any name linked to major drug trafficking gangs. Garrick had felt uneasy at the thought the case would bring them into confrontation with the lowest of the low. Encounters with organised gangs never went well, and the threat of violence was ever present.

A quick tally of the money in the doctor's safe revealed there was a neat £350,000 stashed away for a rainy day. Because of the crisp, yet non-sequential numbers on all the notes, Garrick was in no doubt that Iyer was some kind of mob boss doctor. A trusted advocate who had crossed a line.

He noticed somebody had written a handwritten addendum on the murder board, underneath the photos of Kabir Iyer and his wife, noting they had two children: a daughter who was working in New York, and a son who had started up his own entrepreneurial food tech company. Specially trained grief officers were currently interviewing them, and would no doubt try to coax out any relevant information.

Still, to Garrick's mind, the pieces were a jigsaw cast to the wind, with no indication of what the total picture should be. He wasn't despondent; in fact, he felt a rare thrill, one that he hadn't experienced for a long time. The joy of a case finally stretching out in front of them, with endless possibilities, but as of yet, had no solid destination. It was what had hooked him to police work from the beginning. It was also a relief that this case had no personal connection to himself. Far too many recent cases had seen him mired in a personal character assassination that he had been unaware of. He took a moment away from the board to email his private doctor, hoping she would prescribe something to ease his stress. Her secretary promptly replied, with an appointment the next day.

DC Wilkes crossed over with a list of names which he pinned to the board just under the hospital pictures.

"Who are they?" Garrick asked.

"They're colleagues of Kabir Iyer's we interviewed. We had to do some over Zoom. They're scattered across the country. They all had very nice things to say about him. He was charming, pleasant, and at times overly exuberant. Always making a point of donating to charities and convincing them to part with their cash."

"It takes all kinds..." Garrick muttered.

"He did a sponsored bike ride with them to raise money for Alzheimer's awareness and Children in Need last year. He'd invite them on days out. He was keen on polo, and always invited a bunch of friends down to Cowdray Park to make a day of it. He loved fishing too, and they regularly went out when the weather was good."

Siren's Call

"Sea fishing?" Sean nodded. "Do they happen to mention if he had his own boat?" Garrick tapped the picture of the key on the board.

Sean's brow knitted as he read the notes. It was one of those pieces of evidence that he hadn't had time to ingest. "As it happens, yeah."

Garrick felt a flutter of excitement. In a flurry of phone calls, it took less than an hour for one of Kabir Iyer's friends to reveal the boat was called the Argonaut, and they often set sail from Rye, which was just on the border of East Sussex and Kent.

It took Fanta one rather aggressive conversation with the harbour authority to verify there was such a boat berthed there. It was towards the end of the day when they finally reached the harbour. Garrick arrived with Fanta and as had happened on a previous case, they found parking their unmarked pool car a problem. They wasted 15 minutes to find a space in a local car park only to find out neither of them had any change for the pay and display parking ticket and, for whatever reason, Fanta's parking app wasn't responding.

They crossed to the seafront and found the harbour master's office, where a woman had been impatiently waiting for them. She was in her 50s, plump, with tattooed forearms, wispy grey hair tied in a bun, and a ruddy complexion that enhanced her irritated countenance. She didn't give her name and made the point of looking at her watch as they entered, as she was clearly keen to go home.

"I've seen the fella a few times," she said as she led them down the boardwalk at the water's edge. "But we get all sorts here. He was quite a regular. Always coming down with a bunch of people. Always cheery going out and pissed coming back. I remember at one point he left me with an almost full bottle of posh champers I couldn't finish off. That was nice of him."

She stopped at a boat that gleamed in the evening sun. It was a 34-foot boat, with a shiny upper deck, and a dark blue hull. Fanta had given Garrick the specs on the drive down. It was one of Pursuit's top-end models. The OS 325 Offshore. The enclosed cabin could seat five people, with space on deck for another four or five. It could berth four people, making it an ideal little ocean run around, especially for fishing trips.

"This is the Argonaut."

The harbour master stayed on the pier as Fanta and Garrick stepped on board via a sloping gangplank.

"This must cost a pretty penny," said Garrick.

"Just under 400 grand, brand new."

"Rich toys for crooked boys," Garrick murmured.

They poked around the small cabin space below deck. It was all polished brown wood and immaculate white plastic fittings which had been cleaned to a showroom-ready state. The harbour master had told them most of the high-end boats were maintained by private cleaning crews. Fanta made a note to check them.

The bridge was a small, covered area, with a white luxury swivel-base leather seat, and a sleek black control panel with two large monitors positioned over a bank of switches. Garrick sat in the captain's seat and was amused to find himself bounce a few times before it settled down. He could really imagine himself revving the engine and skipping over the waves.

He looked for a slot on the dashboard and inserted the key they'd retrieved from the safe. A quick quarter turn and the generator powered to life. Navigation screens booted up, and needles on gauges swayed back and forth as they settled down.

"Well, I think it's safe to assume this is his boat," Garrick said.

A navigation screen popped to life with a range of GPS data and a map. There were several abbreviated options that could be tapped, offering further information. Garrick was tempted but hesitated.

"We need a specialist to look at this. Especially the navigational data."

Fanta nodded and started to make a call to bring in the various departments they'd need.

With no hope of the relevant specialists arriving for a day or two, it was all Fanta and Garrick could do to roll some *Police Do Not Cross* tape across the boat's entrance and return home. Although that was something that would take slightly longer as they returned to find their car had been clamped.

Garrick's arm tingled as the pressure increased. He'd been shot at, stabbed, beaten, and singed by explosions. Yet, he judged this as one of the most unpleasant experiences he'd been forced to endure.

The blood pressure cuff expanded to its maximum with a slow hum, and then slowly deflated, releasing the pressure. Dr Rajasekar studied the results with a slightly annoyed grunt.

"I'd hoped that had been third time lucky, but it's third time the same."

Garrick rubbed his sore arm, and she gave him a bemused look.

"I'm sorry, David. We're all out of lollipops. You'll survive."

"So, blood pressure's up," he said in the firmest voice he could manage to try and bring back a semblance of being grown up. "I'm not at all surprised."

"I want to put you on tablets to reduce it. You have hypertension."

"I was hoping for sleeping tablets, or something to calm me down," he said with a thin smile.

"Neither will help with this problem. Hypertension is a silent killer. And at your age..."

"Thanks for the reminder."

"Oddly, when you were under a huge amount of stress, you didn't have it. Maybe that's one for the medical annals."

Garrick finished rolling the arm of his shirt down and fastened the cuffs. "You can write a paper on it, retire and grow famous."

Rajasekar gave a small smile. "I'm hoping to write an entire book on you at some point. I need a retirement plan."

Dr Rajasekar had been his private physician for a couple of years, since his sister died, and the Force had arranged care as his mental health was obviously being affected. Since then, he'd stuck with her, even though the transition from the Force paying the fees to it coming from his own pocket had been an eye-watering experience.

"So, will this be for a couple of months?" Garrick asked.

Rajasekar shook her head. "You'll be on these probably for the rest of your life. There are occasions when people gain a better fitness regime, better diet, and can lose weight, in which case their blood pressure has naturally come down. But it's more of an oddity than the norm."

To some people, that statement might have invoked a feeling of depression. To David Garrick, it was merely another challenge that life was throwing at him.

"Other than that, are you sleeping well?"

"Well, I'm sleeping. Probably better than in the past, but being a father generates its own source of anxiety."

"Is Wendy OK?"

"Oh, a few niggles." He patted his stomach and gave an involuntary laugh. "Niggles. I think it's a northern phrase my mum used to say," he clarified. "Problems, but nothing serious. Just irritants. Apparently, all the usual terrors pregnant women face."

Dr Rajasekar entered his details on the computer as he spoke. "Well, that's good. She should be due soon." Garrick's eyes went wide with the reminder. "How is all this stacking up on you?"

"It's..." He paused. The flippant comment he was about to make evaporated on his lips. "It's given me a sort of new perspective on life, I suppose," he said honestly. "It's making me think... well, all sorts of things about the future."

"Do you have children?" He caught her look, knowing he shouldn't have really asked. She wore a wedding ring, that much he knew. But she wasn't here to see *him* for therapy. After a slightly awkward pause, she laughed and nodded.

"They can be a handful, right? You're about to discover this."

Garrick gave a nervous chuckle. "Blimey, you're supposed to be making me feel OK, not the other way around. You're supposed to be giving me therapy, not making me terrified." He allowed silence to fill the room as he marshalled his thoughts. "I mean, the last few months everything's felt fine, but I've got to admit, lately I've been thinking quite a bit about... Her."

"Your sister?"

He nodded. "And it's in a weird, detached way. Almost like I'm remembering the story of somebody else's life. I don't know. It's hard to explain. I'm guessing that doesn't make much sense."

"Oh, it makes sense. This is how these things go. First of all, there's a period of denial. And then acceptance. And then anger. Finally, acceptance of the situation. It's similar to stages of grieving in some ways. So, it's all perfectly normal. What about hallucinations?"

For a long period, Garrick had suffered terrible, vivid hallucinations, brought on by a swelling on his brain, and then amplified by the vindictive stress he had been placed under.

"Well, I've still been getting headaches. Not like the old migraines. There are certainly no hallucinations. They're thankfully dead and buried." He saw the look on his doctor's face as she reacted to his choice of words, and he immediately regretted them. But she made no comment.

"Well, if you feel ready, I'd like to take you off those medications," Dr Rajasekar said, wobbling her head slightly side to side. "You may feel a little... off-kilter perhaps, because you've been on them for so long. But just make a note of the side effects. If you don't feel well or you think it's affecting your daily routine, then tell me straight away."

"I'm going to go cold turkey?"

"If you like. If you prefer to stay on them, I can extend

the course for a little longer. But it's not healthy to rely on them."

Garrick firmly shook his head. "No, no, no. This is a chapter I most definitely need to bring to an end. Whatever it takes, Doc. Whatever it takes."

Chapter Twelve

The investigation bled into the weekend, with no further progress on identifying the woman. The navigational data from Dr Iyer's ship came in from the Digital Forensic Team towards the end of the day. What Garrick had hoped for was evidence of crossing the Channel, but instead, it revealed the surgeon was a creature of habit. On almost every occasion, he travelled out to his favourite fishing site his friends had confirmed. It was in the North Sea, northeast of Ramsgate and nicely out of the way of the busy shipping channels. He'd found a lively, fertile spot where they always made a good catch.

DCs Harry Lord and Sean Wilkes had begun to liaise with a narcotics team to expose possible connections. They hoped to find a link with Kabir Iyer being a doctor-for-hire for the criminal underground.

The recent fizz of excitement Garrick had been feeling was soon replaced by a malaise.

. . .

Siren's Call

David Garrick found the weekend to be an onslaught of heightened senses as he found himself increasingly aware of Wendy's every minor ache or discomfort. The smile never left her face, but the slightest grunt or gasp when she moved or gently rubbed her swollen stomach had Garrick on his feet and racing back and forth to the kitchen to get a drink or something to eat, whether she wanted it or not.

He found the frantic activity draining, yet he barely slept a wink over the weekend. He'd managed to compartmentalise the case in his mind, so it only occasionally surfaced when he didn't have anything else to occupy him, such as spending time on the toilet where he attempted to leave his phone behind and read a Clive Cussler novel. But that just resulted in him reading an entire chapter without recalling a single word. The rest of his solo time was spent dodging simmering memories of the self-destructive travesty that his sister had unleashed.

By Sunday evening, he felt exhausted. As she went to bed, Wendy kissed him on the forehead.

"I am so glad you're going back to work tomorrow. You need to stop getting under my feet. I'm not made of glass."

That left him feeling somewhat chided and underappreciated before he decided that she probably had a point. He was restless and distracted, and beginning to wonder if it was a result of coming off the medication. Either way, it was a struggle to wake up Monday morning and drive to the office.

As usual, DC Harry Lord was pottering between desks, offering to make cuppas for the whole team. Garrick stood at the murder wall, trying to soak in all the information and hoping a piece of the puzzle would suddenly reveal itself.

However, his increasingly restless mind was drawn towards Harry as he limped around. Whether he realised it or not, their conversation about leaving the force, and Fanta's promotion, had lodged itself into Garrick's subconscious. Perhaps that was the seed for his nagging thoughts about self-doubt.

Fanta was industriously working on her computer, and that somehow further amplified his anxiety. He drew his attention to the board, which, aside from a printed map of Dr Iyer's favourite fishing zones, hadn't changed.

Chib joined him. "I got the last of the interviews from our good surgeon's mates. None of them recall seeing this woman," she indicated the picture of Jane Doe. "Maybe we should reach out to the press?"

Garrick shot her a dark look. Molly Meyers was his pet journalist, a woman whose career had skyrocketed since she had become involved in his life. That hadn't gone unnoticed by other journos, all eager to have a boost up the ladder. Garrick had been swamped by interview requests from across the country. Each journo was eager to befriend him just in case they stumbled over the next great scoop. The fact that none of them had yet chased him for information about the woman on the beach indicated how jaded the press and public had become regarding grim immigrant stories. The truth that this wasn't one such tale still eluded the press corps, and Garrick was keen to keep it that way.

Sean Wilkes added pictures of some notorious gangland leaders that the narcotics division had offered up as possible criminal liaisons.

"None of the operations I spoke to thought any of these gangs had a fixer in Kent," Sean said as he pinned five faces to the board. "And they confirmed the key to having a good doctor on the books, is one that's handy and available at a moment's notice. And doesn't ask any questions. All these blokes," he said, "and her," he added as he pinned the last picture of a glamorous woman to the ranks. The only female in the list of Gangland Kingpins.

Garrick took a cup of herbal tea from DC Lord. "They operate closer to, or in, London, and she's out in Brighton. So that doesn't draw us any closer to anything."

The four of them gazed at the board, eyes searching for patterns or clues.

"It's a bit of a bugger," said Harry.

As they moved closer, Garrick examined the images of the crime bosses. "This one's Russian. There's a surprise. Bulgarian. Albanian. Serbian. And she's a homegrown scumbag.

"It's nice to know women are fighting for parity," Harry quipped. He was still annoyed after attending a mandatory equality workshop for half a day, and that had been a month ago.

Garrick's gaze was drawn to one kingpin. "Serbian..."

Lord nodded. "Yeah. Although they're all equally nasty bastards. What's a feminine bastard?"

"Same," said Chib. "Although–"

Garrick shook his head. "No, no. Not him. Uroš." He tapped the image of the missing man. "Any further news on him? Fanta?"

"Hold on a sec," came her reply as she switched through the computer's database to see if anybody had updated the investigation notes. "Nope. Nothing. He still hasn't turned up, but nobody has reported him missing, either, so there's not a lot we can do."

"We traced him through hospital records, right?"

The words hung on Fanta's lips as she double-checked. "Maidstone. Same hospital Jane Doe met Dr Iyer. It was a DNA match because he had some blood tests there for cholesterol. There is no official record of any liver donation."

"What if he was working for a gang? Got injured... and died. He was a fit to donate to our Jane, which is why we found a lump of him on the boat. All under the knife of our friendly neighbourhood surgeon."

Silence greeted his revelation as the others considered the idea.

"Don't all fall about agreeing now," Garrick snapped tartly.

"It's just as likely he was killed on the boat," said Chib slowly. "Then tossed overboard."

"More likely, if you ask me," Lord added, slurping his tea. "I've got some Hobnobs, if anybody's peckish?" he added.

Garrick was too focused to be sidetracked. "Whatever. Either way, Iyer and Jane Doe are connected. Uroš and Jane Doe are connected, so it's reasonable to assume they're all directly linked."

Fanta read Uroš's report. "His cholesterol was fine. In fact, all his bloods were excellent."

"So why have them tested?"

"Because somebody wanted to see if they'd make a safe transplant." Garrick's inner cop instinct was convinced he was onto something.

DC Wilkes snorted dismissively. "It's a coincidence," he said, returning to his seat.

Garrick was irked. He was surprised by how irritated he felt, and bit back a sharp comment that he was about to direct at his DC. *Careful*, he warned himself. If he was experiencing any side effects from coming off his medication, it wouldn't be a smart idea to allow it to interfere with his work. He knew well enough to trust his team. Yet there was something nagging him, something obvious they were overlooking.

"Sean, go to Uroš's house. See if anybody's seen him locally. And check for any doorbell cameras. See what you can muster."

Sean looked at him with an expression that made it clear he considered the task a pointless punishment. Instead of objecting, he nodded and stood back up from his desk and snatched his jacket from the back of his seat.

"Sure. Why not. I didn't have anything better to do."

He marched from the office. Garrick caught Harry Lord's eye, but his old friend looked sharply away rather than give anything away.

"There's something here," Garrick insisted.

Nobody commented. They all drifted back to their desks, leaving him staring at the sparsely populated boards. He tried not to take their lack of enthusiasm personally, although that was a struggle. Team morale was difficult to maintain on any case that appeared to go nowhere, especially off the back of several high-profile successes that had been both mentally and physically punishing to every one of them. They needed a break soon, or the team's mood would deteriorate. And with one officer heading off for her honeymoon, and two considering leaving, Garrick found it difficult to see how they would be able to navigate smoothly ahead.

It was almost twenty-four hours later when Fanta excitedly sprang from her seat, shattering the strained silence in the office. She and DC Wilkes had been combing through sixty-eight videos he had obtained from various doorbell and home security cameras in Uroš's street. The ubiquitous cameras were now a major tool in fighting crime. Relatively cheap and easy to install, they only started recording when movement was detected, eliminating tedious hours of combing through irrelevant security footage.

The Serbian still hadn't returned home, and none of the neighbours recalled seeing him for almost a fortnight. The old woman next door assumed he had returned home to Novi Sad, to see his family, but calls to the local police there confirmed he had no relations that could be traced.

"We have a suspect!" Fanta yelled across the room as she and Sean swapped a fist-bump. She sat back down as the others crowded around her screen. She replayed the night-time footage, taken at an angle from across the street. Fanta tapped the house they could see. "This *isn't* Uroš's gaff. It's the neighbour. Watch."

A white Range Rover slowly moved down the street at a crawl, before stopping outside Uroš's house, so only the rear half of the vehicle could be seen, the driver just off camera. The taillights blazed too brightly, over-exposing the licence plate number so that it couldn't be read.

"This isn't the breakthrough you may think it is..." muttered Lord.

Fanta shot him an irritated look. "The art of patience will get you everywhere, Harry. Watch and learn."

Garrick tried to hide his amusement when Harry's eyebrows raised indignantly. Harry was about to respond, when a figure stepped around the back of the Range Rover and opened the boot to toss a large military-style satchel in. He slammed the boot and hurried back the way he came. In that moment, there was no mistaking Dr Kabir Iyer as he looked nervously around.

"He's picking Uroš up," said Fanta excitedly. "I bet that's his bag. Look at the date." She called up the metadata on the video clip. It was packed with technical information about the camera, the wi-fi network it was hooked onto, and the date and time. "22:30, three days before the boat came ashore."

They watched as the car pulled away.

"I couldn't make out the plate," Chib commented.

"I tried to run a few screenshots through an image processor," Wilkes said, "to sharpen it up, but the camera quality isn't good enough in the low light."

"And he wasn't driving," said Garrick.

He saw the others exchange a look, before it dawned on Chib. "Because he came and went from the passenger side!" She snapped her fingers. "And Jane Doe left the hospital in a white Range Rover. This is *her* car."

"Well done, you two," Garrick said. "But it's nothing useful right now."

Fanta slowly spun around in her chair and looked archly at him.

"That's why Sean and I went back there this morning and canvassed the other streets for footage." She clicked her fingers. When nothing happened, she sighed and nudged Sean.

"Mmm? Oh. Sorry. Right." He navigated to another set of videos and double-clicked one. It was a corner shop security camera. It showed the Range Rover taking a left at a junction. For the briefest second, the streetlights played over the vehicle as it made the turn. They couldn't identify the driver, but the plate was clear to see.

"Brilliant!" Garrick snapped, drumming his hands on the desk as he felt the thrill of progress. Chib was already darting back to her terminal to access the DVLA database to track the vehicle. Garrick's joy was short-lived.

"It's a cloned plate." Chib sighed deeply as she read. "From a similar vehicle that was written off two months earlier in a crash in Wales."

"Dammit!" Garrick wanted to kick out to vent his frustrations – but curbed his anger. Once again, he was alarmed his emotions were jockeying to take over.

"I'd already checked that," Fanta conceded.

"Like I said. This isn't the breakthrough you think it is, *junior*." DC Lord smirked at Fanta. They had fostered a friendly rivalry over their time together, and it came in handy for disappointments like this. "It's nearly lunch, so–"

"Well, why don't you park your Big Mac backside at your desk? Does anybody else want to come with me to do some actual detecting?"

Garrick couldn't hold back the smile creeping across his face. He recognised his young DC's cocky attitude. "Okay, DC Liu. Where are we going?"

"Sandwich Marina. On a hunch we also found a few cameras around there. Turns out this very vehicle arrived there that night."

The harbourmaster's office was a masterclass in disorganisation. Records were fed into an archaic computer that struggled on an ageing copy of Windows XP, and the backup paperwork lay in piles on every available surface. Garrick didn't know how many legal violations the dazed harbourmaster, Jeremy Campbell, was breaking by not correctly cataloguing the passages of ships in and out of the harbour, but that wasn't his concern. There were armies of civil service bureaucrats who would get to the bottom of that issue. His immediate concern, however, was the hope that the openly nervous Campbell had diligently recorded everything with good old pen and paper, which he assured the police was the case.

It took him 15 minutes to carefully comb through piles of crumpled papers, many of which were stamped by coffee cup rings or the damp that had leaked in through the hole in the roof and smudged the ink.

Garrick spent the time circling around the harbour, hoping to bump into the two fishermen he'd seen before. As fate would have it, they were nowhere to be seen. The chances of ever bumping into them again were slim. Still, their words about ships coming in and out every couple of days rang in his mind. Uroš had gone missing, driven away in a car that had turned up here. Then, a day later, the body of Jane Doe showed up along with the boat and bloodied remnants of the missing Serbian. The English Channel was one of the busiest waterways in the world, so the idea they'd spent two days afloat seemed nonsensical. This left the obvious destination to Europe as the most likely. He'd left DC Lord back at the office, contacting the French and Belgian authorities in his best schoolboy French, which had deteriorated badly - and he'd been bottom of his class so many years ago.

Campbell's voice drifted across the harbour, beckoning Garrick back to the office where he was excitedly wielding a sheet of paper.

"This is it," he declared triumphantly. "The Argonaut, see?" He pointed to the date and time. "It was here for less than 48 hours."

Garrick examined the time stamps on the document. Dr

Iyer's ship had left Rye to pick up Uroš from here. The harbour in Rye was better organised and there were more security cameras. The dates fitted perfectly with the arrival of the Range Rover containing Uroš. So where had he been for the day before being collected at his house, and Iyer turning up here? Garrick's thoughts were drawn to the surgeon's freshly scrubbed home theatre.

"I need to see all your security cameras," Garrick said. The pregnant pause from the harbourmaster caused Garrick to give an involuntary sigh. "Assuming anything around here works."

"Just the gate camera," Campbell said sheepishly. He looked at Fanta. "And you took that already. The rest of them in here haven't worked since, oh, last Christmas, I think." He caught Garrick's eye. "It's not my responsibility, I've reported them, but the management don't want to spend the cash, and poor security is hardly something you want to advertise. After all, this is a commercial business. We've got to bring in punters."

Garrick indicated the paper in his hand and looked at the piles of box files stacked on top of filing cabinets and reaching towards the stained polystyrene tiles. "I want every instance of this boat being here."

Campbell bit his lower lip, and his eyes darted around the office as the scope of the task sunk in. Garrick looked to Fanta. "We'll need a couple of people going through this to make sure our good fellow here doesn't overlook anything vitally important."

Fanta was already several steps ahead. "What a thankless task, but I'm sure DS Okon will be delighted."

"I meant you and Sean."

"I think I'm coming with you, Guv."

Siren's Call

Garrick's brow knitted together. "And where are we going?"

Fanta held up her phone. "There was a text message from Captain Birdseye. France."

Garrick took the phone from her. In the space he'd been talking to Campbell, Fanta had already reached out to her nameless contact in the Navy. His computerised archives had taken seconds to locate the Argonaut's transponder as it left the harbour, and he tracked it halfway across the Channel before the transponder was turned off and the ship vanished.

"Bloody hell, Fanta, anyone would think you're desperate for a promotion. Are you trying to crack this case entirely on your own?"

"Why break a habit..."

"They could be headed anywhere. France is a big country, you know."

"I have some thoughts on that."

Garrick returned her phone. "I'm absolutely sure that's true, Fanta."

At 8 o'clock the following morning, Garrick found himself as the permanently nervous passenger in Fanta's Polo as she crawled along the platform of the Eurotunnel, following a Mercedes in front. As they turned through the open shuttered door of the slightly grubby train carriage, a marshal in a fluorescent coat encouraged them onwards with a wave. Fanta took the tight turn inside and then drove up a steep ramp onto the first floor of the double-decker rail carriage.

Despite all his years living in Kent, Garrick had never taken the Eurotunnel before. And even with Fanta at the wheel, he was enjoying the experience. The long carriage stretched out before them, and he felt he was in a science fiction TV show he'd enjoyed long ago as a kid in Liverpool.

Every few metres, he caught sight of Kent's rolling hills through the small side windows, and at one point he saw the magnificent chalk horse etched on the side of a hill. Though sadly it wasn't a Neolithic wonder, but a marketing stunt when the tunnel had opened in 1994.

Fanta pulled up as the car in front stopped. Another marshal indicated she should edge forwards, which she did so with an audible whimper, convinced that she was going to bump the Mercedes. A sharp hand signal from the jacketed warden gave her time to stop, inches from collision, and he indicated she should lower her window.

"Keep your window down and handbrake on," he said with a monotony drilled in by repeating this statement every day, before moving to the car behind them.

Fanta cut the engine and relaxed. "I love France," she said.

Garrick couldn't work out if it was fate, coincidence, or bad luck that had stuck him here with Fanta rather than any of the other officers on the team. Chib had pointed out that she still didn't have her passport back. Then Garrick had discovered none of the police pool cars were insured for European travel. He had to resort to Fanta's personal vehicle. Something that he loathed at the best of times. Her Volkswagen had been pimped up to boy racer standards with an overly loud exhaust, go-faster stripes, and LEDs that blazed to life under the chassis of the car to illuminate the road beneath. They were all hideous additions, and Garrick couldn't understand why Fanta was so happy to be a reject from *The Fast and the Furious*.

Siren's Call

Then there was the annoying fact that Fanta was bilingual, in fact more than that—she could speak passable French, Spanish, and fluent Mandarin. Garrick shook his head as she spoke. He was no longer surprised by his DC's abilities and level of ambition.

He used the manual lever to recline the seat back a little bit and shuffled to get comfortable for the 35-minute train ride ahead.

"Exciting, isn't it?" said Fanta enthusiastically.

It felt as though they hadn't been parked for 10 minutes before the hills outside slowly drifted past as the train accelerated with barely any sense of motion. The safety tannoy sounded throughout the carriage, replaying instructions in both English and French.

As the windows turned black when they plunged into the tunnel proper, Garrick was already asleep, with Fanta still talking. It felt as though he had merely blinked as he emerged from a muddle of vivid memories of a dream he couldn't recall.

"Look," Fanta pointed out, "we're already in France."

Garrick blinked in the bright sunlight outside. His eyes adjusted so he could make out the flat farmers' fields of the *Pas-de-Calais* region. His phone had already switched to the French SFR network, and he cringed at the thought of the roaming charges that would be inflicted upon him.

Fanta was grinning ear to ear as the train stopped at the Calais terminal and a few minutes later, the safety doors separating the carriages rose, putting Garrick in mind of a missile launch tube on a submarine or maybe a spaceship. Engines rumbled to life, and the convoy in front of them rolled forward. Fanta joined in, her own highly tuned engine screaming like a lion in the confined space. She didn't seem particularly embarrassed by this as they trundled down an exit ramp and onto the platform of Calais, France.

"The right! The right! The right!" Garrick hollered with increasing urgency, flailing his hand in front of Fanta's face as she jinked the wheel.

"God, I know," she growled, her knuckles gripping the steering wheel so tightly they turned white. "I can drive."

It was completely against the evidence Garrick was witnessing with his own eyes, as Fanta weaved across the roads of France with as much respect as she gave them in England.

Garrick blew out a long, pent-up breath as she settled back into the correct lane. "I tell you what, you keep your eyes on the road, I'll keep my eyes on the GPS, and that way, through teamwork, we won't crash and die," he suggested.

Fanta pulled a face but didn't say anything. Since leaving the station, it was only a short hop to the neighbouring *Cité Europe*, where DC Lord had managed to arrange a meeting with a French counterpart. It turned out to be a huge retail outlet on the edge of Calais. They pulled into the car park. Being early on a Wednesday morning, there were plenty of spaces for Fanta to park without turning the situation into a demolition derby. They headed towards the Columbus Café to meet the detective. Fanta held up her phone, comparing the handful of people in there to the photo she'd been emailed. The detective was sitting in the corner. She was an elegant, slender woman in her late thirties, five foot six, with dark brown bobbed hair, wide chocolate-coloured eyes, and a Mediterranean complexion. She extended her hand.

"Detective Celine Agon," she said in perfect English, enhanced by a certain French accent.

Garrick gaped slightly, taken in by a sudden stereotype –

a beautiful French detective hewn from corny TV movies. He found his voice and shook her hand.

"Detective Chief Inspector Garrick. Pleasure to meet you." Garrick pulled himself together, but his cheeks were already flushing crimson. He caught Fanta's piercing sidelong glance. "Call me David, and this is my Detective Constable, Fanta."

Detective Agon's eyebrows knitted quizzically together. "Fanta? I have never heard this name before."

"My father had a vivid imagination and a poor grasp of English," Fanta replied. "Shall I get us some drinks?"

After a brief diversion to buy two ham and Emmental baguettes, a coffee for Fanta and Detective Agon, and a raspberry-infused herbal tea for Garrick, they sat in a quiet corner.

"The detective was a little confused on the phone," Agon began.

"Ah, that would be his French," Garrick said apologetically. "Luckily, your English is better than his." He gave a charming smile and heard Fanta *tut*.

"He explained your case and sent through some notes. You suspect trafficking, France to England? Possibly a Serbian gang?"

"Our theory is they're trafficking drugs, maybe."

Detective Agon nodded. "Here we are at the hub of illegal boat crossings to Britain. Immigration is a touchy subject on both sides of the channel, *non*?"

"Unfortunately so," said Garrick, not wishing to be drawn into a political conversation the French loved so much.

Agon continued. "What is lesser known, maybe, is that immigration is scratching the surface of the real problems.

They're a perfect conduit for all crimes: human trafficking, drugs, guns, terrorism. You name it, the migrants will be used for it. They're the victims."

"None of our leads are illegal immigrants. But as you say, they're used for these things."

"There were some particular points in the case notes your detective sent through that caught my attention."

"Oh, I'm glad about that," said Garrick with another charming smile that he instantly regretted.

"He said you suspect an organised drugs trafficking gang, using these routes. This happens a lot," Agon nodded. "But I think from the details you have given me, that you are wrong."

Garrick exchanged a puzzled look with Fanta. "What do you mean?"

Celine Agon gazed contemplatively into the corner of the room before giving a small shrug. "I think it's best for you to see and deduce for yourself. I don't wish to influence your investigation. Perhaps the best course of action, once, you have finished your baguette, is to see for yourself." She met Garrick's gaze with an intense look that made him glance away quickly and focus on his sandwich, reminding himself that he was about to be a father to a wonderful woman back in England.

Chapter Thirteen

Detective Agon had been horrified when she had seen Fanta's car, so she suggested that they all take her dark grey Nissan Qashqai, which wouldn't stand out. They drove away from the motorway and towards the coast. Even before they saw the sign for the town of Sangatte, Garrick could already see lines of tents filled with immigrants from around the globe. Despite his prejudice of expecting a disorganised, rough and tumble Wild West frontier, there appeared to be some organisation to the camp. The groups of people, mostly young, weren't just men, but women and children. Most of them were laughing and joking, despite the scars of whatever horrors they'd endured etched across their faces.

Consigned to the back seat, Fanta muttered a low, "Oh my God," as she took in the scale of the camp. "There are thousands of them."

"They keep being cleared. Destroying the camps to save the village, but they keep coming back." Celine Agon carefully drove them through the town. "They come from around the world constantly. These days the political situation makes things more difficult. When you were part of the EU, part of Schengen, they could be returned to their point of entry. Greece or further. Instead, they are now returned right back here to try again and again and again."

"What is it about France that's so bad they want to leave here and come to England?" said Garrick. He'd meant it as a joke, but his comment came out dry and devoid of humour.

Agon flashed a wry smile. "That's exactly what I say!"

She pulled over to the side of the road and parked the car near a cluster of makeshift tents and corrugated metal and wood structures that formed a basic supply shop that served the community.

"Is it safe?" Fanta said with a trace of alarm.

"Oh, they know me."

They exited the car, which Garrick noted she immediately locked, and walked towards a temporary supply store run by a pair of notably white French people. They gave a rapid exchange in French, and a huge man covered in tattoos, his long greasy hair pulled back in a ponytail, nodded and crossed to Garrick and Fanta to shake their hands.

"I believe you want to talk to some people," he said with a thick Gallic accent.

"If that's okay," said Garrick.

The man smiled and gestured around. In any other situation, he would have fitted perfectly as the thuggish leader of a Hell's Angels gang. Yet here, he was distributing food and water to the needy.

"People like to talk. I think Celine has a few specific people in mind. This way."

Crouched in a corner, eating rice from a dish with their fingers and wrapped in heavy blankets despite the relatively mild day were three thin, fatigued individuals with dead eyes, who looked as if life had been squeezed from them.

"This is Benny," the man gestured. "He's from Somalia." The man had almost midnight black skin that highlighted his white teeth, which he flashed in greeting. "Churni here, from Bangladesh." A woman who kept her hair tied in a scarf gave a small, frail nod but remained expressionless. "And Karrar, from Iraq."

Detective Agon spoke in slow, clear English. "They all agreed to talk to us." With a sly smile, she passed two packets of cigarettes to Benny, who snatched them into the folds of his blanket with snake-like speed.

Celine indicated Fanta and Garrick. "My friends here wish to know about what *really* happens here." She looked seriously at Fanta and Garrick in turn. "These people have their own harrowing reasons for leaving their homeland, but they are not relevant for you. It is all the same theme of persecution and desperation. Of walking part way around the globe without money or food, in search of something better than what they had left behind. That is the unifying connection. Their inherent fight for life, and the invisible barriers between countries that form the so-called civilised world. In prehistoric times, one could have wandered the entire globe without question. You could even walk from here to Kent, across the Land Bridge, because there was no sleeve."

She caught Garrick's frown. "That's what we call the water," she gestured.

"The English Channel," said Fanta.

Agon's shoulders tensed. "Only you English call it the *English* Channel. I am sure it doesn't belong to you."

Fanta wisely remained silent.

"It takes a lot of money to cross over into England," the detective continued. "Gangs operate from here, specifically to ferry people on boats." She raised a finger to stop Garrick from interrupting. "But that is not my area. And that is not why we are here. This region is a network of organised crime. The organisers who move people over on the boats are not the same people who deal drugs or guns. There is money to be made for being a courier. But the risks are high. Hundreds of people die making this crossing. The drug cartels are not concerned about them. They are only concerned when somebody drowns, and their shipment is lost. Life is meaningless, but losing money is unforgivable. It is not a good business to use these people as drug mules."

Garrick hadn't considered it that way before. Now his mind was racing as to why Detective Agon was showing an interest in their case, while at the same time shooting down their main line of investigation.

"How do these people find money to cross? How much is it? £5,000 to make a journey? It's ridiculous," said Garrick.

Fanta gave out a low whistle. "Wow, even Eurotunnel was cheaper than that. And I thought that was a bit of a rip-off."

"I suppose the crime rate is sky-high here," said Garrick.

Agon gave a sad smile. "Of course. People see them all as thieves, but most of the crime is petty. Money for food, medicine, essentials. They're not bank robbers holding up armed guards for thousands of Euros they need to cross. They must use what they have." She looked meaningfully at Benny. "Please show them."

The Somali put down his plate of rice and gave a sombre nod. He moved the blanket, revealing a grubby Manchester United top underneath, and stood. He hoisted up the shirt, revealing an ugly scar across his abdomen. The flesh was dark and discoloured, and seeping pus.

"I don't understand," said Fanta, looking between Agon and the man.

"They all have similar wounds. They took part of his liver."

.Garrick did understand, and he felt sick at the implications. "Organ harvesting," he said quietly.

Benny yanked his shirt back down and quickly sat, pulling the blanket back over him as he shivered. He continued eating, ignoring the conversation floating around him.

Celine nodded. "Exactly."

Garrick studied Fanta's face as the implications set in for her too.

"For money?" she asked flatly.

Garrick nodded. "You know, I'd heard about it, but... I always thought it was some kind of joke students put around to pay for their gap year."

"It's a very real trade," Celine Agon said. "Kidney, liver, lung, anything is for sale. They make enough money to try for a new life across the Channel. What else do they have?"

"That's utterly sick," said Fanta.

"*Oui*. Sick and brutal. There's a very specific gang behind this. Your drug cartels, your weapons traffickers, they all think these people are beneath them." She gestured to the three refugees. "But even they think organ harvesters are people to be avoided. The violence behind trading cocaine is a by-product to protect their merchandise. For harvesters, these people *are* the merchandise."

"Who would buy a body part?" said Fanta, struggling to process the new situation.

"Rich people who are ill," said Agon. "I do not mean millionaires. Even the affluent middle classes. There are limits that even private health can't support. There are waiting lists for the correct match. If you need a new kidney, for example, it must be a match. It must be healthy. Imagine if you're turning blind, you need a cornea implant. You will have to wait for a volunteer."

Fanta frowned. Garrick gave a dark chuckle.

"I think by volunteer she means wait for a rainy day and a biker going far too fast. They're the usual first in line to donate organs."

Celine pressed on. "Just as these people are desperate for a new life, so are the people on the other side of the equation. Desperate to rid themselves of their illness, of their disease, and wealthy enough to take advantage of the poor."

Fanta was disgusted. "We're not animals."

Celine gave a laugh. "Of course we are animals. We are no different. And these harvesters do not see a difference between a horse going to market," she gestured towards the woman, "or a woman who genetically matches somebody desperate for a new lung. One that when grafted would not be rejected by the body. We are valuable creatures."

"How valuable?" asked Garrick.

"Raw elements inside us, iron, zinc, copper, maybe 600 Euros. A kidney, a quarter of a million. A liver, half a million. A heart, a million at least. It is illegal in every country. Except Iran," she added with a shrug.

Fanta was shocked. She caught Garrick staring at her.

"Why are you looking at me like that?"

"I'm eying you up for my retirement plan."

They thanked the three refugees and walked towards Detective Agon's car. Garrick felt the overwhelming urge to try to help the refugees by offering them money, but fought back from this rare charitable impulse. Taking the chance to cross the Channel, breaking laws and risking their lives was a lethal gamble. Even if they did survive the crossing, the chances were high they would be caught and deported back to the place they were fleeing from. And on top of that, now risked the chance of dying due to a less than sanitary operation, as Celine confirmed when they reached her car.

"I don't think Benny will survive much longer," she confided. "The hospitals won't take him. We have a doctor who has seen him but refuses further treatment. I think the operation made him afraid of doctors."

They leaned against her car to take in the bleak surroundings.

"How widespread is this?" Garrick asked.

"A single gang. In this region at least. It's such a dark art, there is very little competition."

"I suppose the rival competition could end up being the one on sale."

"Yes. Harvesting is my area of investigation. For some time, we have known of a gang operating between our shores. And I suspected a specialist surgeon was based in the United Kingdom."

"Our dead Dr Iyer."

Celine Agon nodded. "The surgery you found fits very much within their operational structure. And you have closed it down."

Fanta was struggling with the new reality. "I understand why these poor people are desperate for money, but how does Uroš fit into this? He was legally in the UK."

"Chib uncovered his substantial debts. Loans to cover his studies," said Garrick, as he tried to remember what his DS had told him. "I bet he was under pressure to pay them off. I also think if we dig deep enough, we'll find out he *didn't* come over here legally. Maybe he was paying for false documents that proved he could stay? That costs a lot of money."

Celine nodded. "You are right. It is not just immigrants. People across France, across the world, and that includes England, volunteer themselves for this barbarity."

Fanta had gone pale, and despite the cool breeze, a sheen of sweat covered her brow.

"Are you feeling okay?" Garrick asked her.

"I feel a bit sick, guv." The bravado and confidence she routinely portrayed was wearing to her very soul. Garrick resisted a friendly pat on the shoulder, fearing it would seem a little too paternal in front of the French detective. He focused back on Celine.

"You said there was one gang?" When she nodded, Garrick felt his theory about warring rivals start to crumble. "Are you sure?"

"We had a very thorough investigation into them. They are very ruthless. We placed an undercover operative, a... a friend of mine." She gave a long pause as she became choked with emotion. Garrick recognised the internal fight taking place inside as she mastered her turmoil. She succeeded, drew in a sharp breath. "He was killed in the line of duty when they found out his identity. His body was left in a public square in Calais. Dissected." She fell silent and stared at the floor. "They were sending a message to us. And then the whole operation," she snapped her fingers, "every lead we had vanished like smoke. Not that they stopped. They are like cockroaches, scampering into the shadows. If this is what I think it is, you've given us the biggest breakthrough I could have dreamed of in the last year. You need to see something else."

Wimereux was a seaside commune south of Calais, nestled on a pleasant sandy coastline. Just driving through, past the brasserie and village square, Garrick was taken by what a nice quintessential French break it would make for him and Wendy, if it were not for the dark shadow of human organ harvesting.

Detective Celine Agon drove them to a farm that was just over a kilometre away from the village itself. There was a sense of abandonment as they arrived. Not a soul stirred, and even the birds seemed to avoid the area. The countryside around them was deathly silent. Strands of weather-beaten police tape attached to the gate whipped in the breeze as they entered the grounds.

"This was owned by a pig farmer. His family had owned the area for generations," Celine explained. "The current owner, Sebastian, turned out to have a desire to make more money than the family business could."

She led them through a series of barns, towards a large well-maintained unit that was closed with a heavy padlock. She fished out a key, unlocked it. Then she braced her foot against the frame, putting her entire body weight into sliding the door open with a grunt. She gestured inside. Garrick and Fanta followed, stepping into a disturbingly familiar scene.

Pushing plastic drapes aside, it was almost a carbon copy of Dr Kabir Iyer's home medical facility. All the tools had been removed, but a steel operating table, refrigerator and cupboards remained. It was a completely sealed unit, lit by bright halogen bulbs, which came on with a slow electrical thump when Celine flicked the switches.

"Look familiar?" she said, cocking her head.

"Sadly," Garrick said.

"So, the other half of the operation you uncovered in England. This was their base here. We arrested the farmer, but not the surgeon. Of course, the farmer denies knowing anybody else involved. That is the price you pay for involving yourself with traffickers. He is no longer safe. His family are no longer safe. Silence is guaranteed by death.

Fanta shivered. "Do you think our surgeon is the same man?"

Celine nodded. "The photograph your colleague sent through confirmed it. Dr Kabir Iyer was the butcher of Wimereux." She circled round the table. "The unfortunate souls who volunteer for surgery are often not the healthiest of specimens. Oh, their internal organs will do for the most part. But physically, they are often not up to making a full recovery. Like Benny." She gave them a sad look. "That's why I don't feel guilty for plying him with cigarettes."

"Do you have figures on the mortality rate?" Garrick asked.

Celine shook her head. "Nothing precise, which is why your Serbian candidate would have been of great value to them. A fit, healthy man. And he stood every chance of surviving. They are not interested in leaving a trail of bodies. They can be found. The living can just fade away. But, as I said, many are weak and perish." She drummed her fingers on the stainless-steel surface of the operating table. "We found many remains here." She gestured in a vague direction where Garrick recalled seeing a line of empty pigsties. "Pigs eat almost anything. Almost. They don't eat many bones. We have identified 15 different people, and we think that is, I don't know what the English phrase is, a small part of something big."

"The tip of the iceberg," said Garrick.

Fanta clarified in French. "*Il y a anguille sous roche.*" She caught Garrick's frown. "It's something about eels. Same meaning."

Celine was impressed. "Your French is beautiful."

The compliment was enough to put Fanta back on her mental feet. "This is the operation you brought down a few months ago. And we've stopped the one in the UK."

Celine wagged a finger. "I think so. Which is why we find ourselves at a critical time for this operation. As you can imagine, setting up something like this is not simple. It's much more specialist than a mere drug factory. Medical facilities, even ones like this, require a level of cleanliness. Even if the victim is weak, a contaminated organ is worthless. Closing both theatres will stop their ability to do business until they build another."

Garrick's mind was racing through the facts pinned to the murder board.

"One gang. That means Iyer's death was not a rival retaliation. And with him dead, they'd be severely damaging their own business."

Fanta welcomed the chance to take her mind off the practicalities of human organ harvesting.

"What if it's an internal struggle? Like a battle for leadership?"

"And Iyer got on the wrong side..." Garrick mulled the idea. He wasn't sure it held water, but maybe DC Liu was onto something. What do you have on the gang?"

Celine gave a particularly Gallic exclamation, and her

hands splayed out helplessly. "Very little. They operate behind others. Sometimes the organ shipments are delivered amongst weapons, or drugs. Woven into a courier's shipment, sometimes even without their knowledge. Occasionally they are given to refugees. I know one woman who was forced to carry her own kidney as she crossed into England. She didn't make it. The cool box with the organ in, did."

The picture Detective Agon was painting was increasingly ugly and ruthless.

"What about the woman we found on the beach?"

Celine's brown eyes lit up. "It is her who caught my interest. I have no record of her, but I have seen this woman before."

"Operating with the gang?"

"Yes. But I am not sure how. Not as a courier, but as somebody who appeared to have *authority*."

"But not enough authority to stop her from being killed by her own people and tossed overboard," said Fanta.

Celine pursed her lips. "She is an enigma, Detective Garrick. One I hope we can crack together." She seemed to reach a decision and took a small black box from her inside jacket pocket. She offered it to Garrick. "This is all the information I have on their operation. I hope you can find things in there I have missed."

With a frown, Garrick took it. It was a small 3-inch external hard drive. The plastic case weighed nothing in his hand, but from the gravitas in Celine's voice, it was worth more than the Crown Jewels. Garrick thanked her and stashed it in his Barbour's inside pocket. The odd nature of the transaction passed without comment. There was a formal avenue established for sharing information, but one the French Detective wished to bypass for her own reasons.

With firm promises of close cooperation, Garrick and Fanta said goodbye to Detective Agon. It was made even more disheartening when he was forced to decline her dinner invitation in order to catch the Eurotunnel back home.

As Fanta drove them back to the terminal, Garrick was so lost in thought about the lucky escape from spending any more time with the French detective, that he failed to criticise Fanta's driving, even when she strayed into the left-hand lane and almost ran a local off the road.

Chapter Fourteen

DCI David Garrick had long ago learned to trust his gut; forged from years of instinct from dealing with the most devious minds who twisted truth and fact into lies that were literally at the heart of life and death. And at this moment, his gut was vying for attention, insisting that something didn't feel right.

The journey back to the Calais Eurotunnel Terminal was conducted entirely in silence. Fanta and Garrick were lost in their own uncomfortable thoughts as they waited in the car park outside the terminal building before deciding to head inside because, despite the grim details of human organ harvesting, Fanta craved a burger and fries, and they both needed something to wet their whistle.

The terminal was as bland as the food, so Garrick didn't eat and was forced to watch Fanta slowly chewing her way through the lukewarm food. Boarding Group T was called, and they returned to their car and passed through both French and British customs checks, with the French waving them through without a glance, and only the British officers checking their credentials. This time they found themselves on the lower deck, parking behind a Luton van that just about fitted within the vertical space.

Garrick extracted the portable hard drive from his pocket and gazed at it thoughtfully. "What is on this that she couldn't email it to us, do you think?"

Fanta had reclined her seat a little and shuffled to get comfortable. "I don't know, but she sounded a little paranoid to me."

"If the harvesters killed her colleague, can you blame her?" Garrick's own ex-DS had been killed in the line of duty. They hadn't been working together at the time, but the scars from a severed kinship still stung.

Fanta flashed Garrick a small grin. "I think paranoia is a good thing. Our little team has run on pure paranoia, and look at us."

Despite himself, Garrick gave a dark chuckle. Ever since he'd been the target for an internal investigation, which planted DS Chib within the unit, they'd all had more than their fair share of internal politics, bickering, and paranoia. The net result had made them all stronger and vigilant.

There was a 16-minute delay before the train gently pulled out of Calais and rolled across the flat, featureless farmland. By the time they plunged into the darkness of the tunnel, Fanta was fast asleep with her mouth open. Despite his fatigue, Garrick knew he'd be unable to nap. There were too many questions and anxieties rattling around his skull. He hadn't eaten since the baguette in France but still didn't feel hungry. They were all familiar signs he recognised as being stress-induced.

Still, he tried to get comfortable in Fanta's unnecessarily sporty bucket seat, and swore to himself – not for the umpteenth time – that this was the last time he'd get into this car. With nothing but darkness outside, there was only the occasional sense of movement due to the background thrum of the train and the occasional, gentle sway side-to-side. Passengers left their cars to stretch their legs and search for the toilets, but soon their numbers dwindled. Garrick couldn't recall many vehicles waiting to board, so he wouldn't be surprised if the train was less than half full.

Despite everything, he felt himself relax and his mind began to wander onto Wendy. He hadn't heard from her all day, and he amused himself imagining what she was doing. Probably lying on the sofa watching TV and sleeping. If it wasn't for his gnawing anxiety, he would have been asleep so wouldn't have seen the rear door on the van in front of him crack open.

Whoever was inside had anticipated the door to open wider. Instead, it touched against Fanta's bonnet, forcing a small, dark-skinned man to breathe in as he slipped through the narrow gap. With no space, he splayed unceremoniously across the bonnet. Garrick blinked in surprise. Had he slipped illegally onboard and was now making his escape? The man's taut expression was now marred by a shade of embarrassment. The next thing Garrick registered was the automatic pistol in the man's hand. The barrel was tipped with a large silencer that almost doubled the gun's length.

Garrick acted on pure instinct. His hand snatched to release the handbrake while at the same time throwing his entire body weight to the left, pushing open his door with his other hand. The man raised the pistol but was unprepared for the train's gentle rocking - and the fact Garrick had released the handbrake. Fanta's car rolled backwards with a soft *crump* against the Mini Cooper parked behind them.

Siren's Call

Swearing rose from the Mini's driver as he got out to inspect the damage. Garrick was now out of the vehicle. With one foot on the door sill, he propelled himself at his distracted assailant. His hand snatched the man's wrist as he swung the gun towards Garrick, firing an uncoordinated volley of near-silent shots that shattered the windscreen and woke Fanta from her deep sleep. She threw open her door to roll out of the car.

Garrick stretched his left arm, searching for the man's throat. His fingers wrapped around coarse stubble, and he clenched as tightly as he could – slamming the gunman's his head backward as he snatched the gun and yanked in the opposite direction. The man's face turned scarlet, and he choked. Yet despite Garrick's obvious size and weight advantage, his assailant was built like a bulldog. He tensed the ripped muscles in his neck to combat the throttling.

With a wild yell that reverberated through the carriage, Garrick repeatedly slammed the man's head against the Luton van's closed door with such fury that the tinted safety glass cracked.

The man popped another shot - and the train's side window shattered. The air pressure in the carriage painfully popped everybody's ears as an 80-mph gale blew inside. It was enough to confound the gunman. Garrick jerked his knee up for a painful, bollock-crushing blow. That took the man's breath away. He rolled off the bonnet and fell between the increased gap between Fanta's car and the van.

On his knees, his face red with anger and hate, he had just enough focus to raise the gun inches from Garrick's face.

Garrick froze. He had been close to death on many occasions. But this felt different. The shot was point-blank. The bullet could not miss.

Death was inevitable.

In this final split-second moment, all he could think about was Wendy and his unborn daughter.

Neither man noticed that Fanta was back on her feet. She floundered against the wall and pulled the emergency stop lever down with force. Almost immediately, the train aggressively braked. Every vehicle rocked forwards – held in place by their handbrakes.

Except Fanta's Polo.

Her car shot forward with force, crushing into the gunman's ribcage. With an eye-watering crunch of bone, he immediately dropped the gun, and convulsed. His eyes rolled in his skull and blood trickled from between his lips.

Not that Garrick saw the horror. Inertia hurled him against the Luton's door. But he heard screams from behind as passengers witnessed everything. He fought to recover as the driver's side of the van opened. Another man, with a swarthy Algerian complexion, jumped out and fired wild shots at Fanta as she hunkered against her car. The man didn't wait. He kicked open the fire door leading to the carriage in front and bolted through it.

Fanta reacted quicker than her boss, snatching the original gunman's discarded pistol - she took a pot shot at the fleeing man, missing wildly. It was enough for Garrick to pull himself together and leap off the bonnet. He snatched the pistol from Fanta and charged in pursuit of the gunman.

The train had ground to a halt in the tunnel. In the next carriage the second gunman's progress was impeded by people exiting their cars and blocking the access way. An emergency announcement instructing them to remain in their vehicles went unheeded. The man wildly shouldered people aside, waving his gun as an added menace.

Siren's Call

Garrick pinballed through the people, but had a slightly clearer route from terrified passengers pressing themselves against the wall to avoid the two crazy men. He saw his prey disappearing through the fire doors, into the next carriage. By the time he caught up, the man had opened the emergency door and jumped out into the main running tunnel.

Garrick didn't slow his pace as he followed the man into the darkness. There was just enough light to clamber down the few steps of an access ladder, and he felt solid concrete beneath his feet. His eyes became adjusted to the dimness and a series of emergency lights illuminating the long tunnel. The train had stopped on the flat section, but ahead he could see the line of lights make an upturn as the track began its ascent back to the surface.

He flinched as a gunshot rang out. He crouched and took aim at the fleeing man who was a hundred yards ahead. They were 250 feet under the seabed, so Garrick had no fear of shooting through the roof and drowning them all, but he still hesitated, buying the gunman enough time to duck through a side door.

Cursing how unfit he was, Garrick ran in pursuit. The would-be assassin had pushed through an emergency door in the side of the tunnel. It was slowly swinging back closed on noisy hinges. Garrick remembered the layout of the tunnel from a training day many years earlier. There were three tunnels. Two running tunnels for the trains, separated by a central emergency service tunnel that stretched from one country to the other and used by maintenance and emergency vehicles.

Pushing through the door, Garrick stepped into a dimly lit narrow passage. Emergency arrows coaxed him onwards. He just caught sight of the man disappearing through another fire door the end of the passage, and gave chase into the service tunnel.

The central service tunnel was well lit and stretched in both directions as far as he could see. The road was smooth and flat; the concrete panelled walls curving upwards to a nest of hanging conduits and pipes. It was just about wide enough for the specially built service vehicles that could carry two people side-by-side – and there was absolutely no cover for the fleeing gunman to hide. A revelation that struck him as he came to a complete stop just yards ahead. He hunched over, with his hands on his knees as he caught his breath. The silenced pistol was still in his hand. Garrick raised his gun; hands trembling from fear and exhaustion.

"Police, stop!" The schoolboy French rattled somewhere in his head. "*Arrêtez!*" he added, hoping that was the right word. "Put the gun down!"

The man didn't relinquish his firearm but slowly turned to look at Garrick. He had been expecting the hardened face of a killer. He hadn't expected to see the lost, bewildered expression of a man in his twenties, with tears streaming down his face.

"Put the weapon down, mate."

The man stared at him. Worried that the message wasn't getting through, Garrick attempted a mime, stopping short of throwing his own weapon aside. Still the man didn't react, although the tears increased as he looked at the gun in his own hands.

"Gun. Down. Now." Garrick enunciated as clearly as he could, indicating to his own gun and the floor.

The man sucked in a long deep breath and met Garrick's gaze. Then he nodded. The utter despair on his face was unmistakable. He raised his gun and pushed it against his temple.

"No!" Garrick cried.

The soft punt of air from the silencer barely registered in the tunnel. His body dropped like a dead weight straight down to the floor. Garrick knew he would never unsee the man blowing his own brains out.

Chapter Fifteen

It took eleven hours for Garrick to leave the tunnel. By the time he had heard the emergency service sirens whooping as they entered the tunnel from the English side, it was still several minutes before the vehicles reached him, and he was forced to flag them down to avoid hitting the dead gunman.

On board the train, the first gunman who'd been wedged between the car and the van was in critical condition. He was alive only because of the efforts of an off-duty nurse, who'd managed to ease the bleeding, and in doing so cover herself entirely in the man's blood. He was extracted from the train and placed into an ambulance in the service tunnel to be whisked back to the surface.

When it was deemed no other passengers were injured, and the damage to the train carriage was minimal, the train eventually continued to limp onwards to Folkestone. Several British Transport Police officers stayed onboard at the crime scene and took statements.

Fanta was spattered with dry blood specks from the

injured gunman and was keeping a brave face despite the shock she felt. Donning latex gloves from the back of Fanta's car, they examined the van with the Transport Officer. On the front seat was a plastic folder with both their pictures printed out in colour.

"These are from our warrant cards," Fanta pointed out.

Her eyes met Garrick's and then flicked to the Transport officers. They were convinced the hit was the work of the harvesting gang Detective Agon had warned them about. If they had access to British police files, then their tendrils stretched very far.

It wasn't until they reached Folkestone and discovered a media circus had gathered at the outskirts of the train station. A news helicopter circled overhead, as stories of a terror incident on the Eurotunnel ran rampant across social media.

Despite it being four in the morning, Garrick wasn't too surprised to find Superintendent Malcolm Reynolds waiting for them at an unmarked police car parked across the platform.

"When I heard there was a major international mess on the Eurotunnel, who did I think of?"

Garrick feigned a smile. "I thought you'd just come to pick us up, sir, since Fanta's car is being impounded."

"I can't tell you how much of a mess this is, David. And discharging a firearm," he shook his head in disbelief as he looked at Fanta. "I've already seen the video footage of what went on inside the carriage. DC Liu, you are not authorised to use a firearm. You've had no training."

Fanta looked at him in surprise. She wasn't one to be intimidated by her superiors. "Are you joking? He had a gun!"

Garrick made a face, silently trying to shut her up.

"I advise you to shut up, detective," Reynolds snapped. "I'm breaking every rule not to suspend you right now!"

The colour visibly drained from Fanta's face, and she opened her mouth to snap back.

Garrick quickly interjected, "Guv, she was protecting lives."

Reynolds held up his hand. "And you better listen too. You should *both* be suspended, bearing in mind it looks like we've just had a foiled hit against two of our officers—yes, I've already read the statement you gave. Luckily, email travels faster than this train. That puts you at risk. And people around you."

"They had pictures from our warrant cards," said Fanta. She was trying to be firm and composed, but the crack in her voice gave her anxiety away.

"I've instructed Chib to investigate just what the hell is going on and interview that gunman. I don't want you two near him in case you led the press into this mess." He scowled at Garrick. "They follow you like flies on shit. Do I make myself clear?"

"Vividly."

"I need to keep this as clean as possible. You're both forbidden to talk to the press. Okay?" He glowered at Garrick. "If I so much as hear Molly Meyers or any of her wannabes suddenly have an inside scoop on this, you *will* be suspended."

Garrick inflated his cheeks and then spat out a mouthful of air, along with it the tensions he was suppressing. All those months of yoga hadn't been for nothing. "We're dealing with an international gang who have got no morals and a healthy respect for violence," he stated. "This is not a pair of kids up to no good, and it's not a terrorist attack. We've contacted a detective in France who–"

"Detective Agon is now missing," Reynolds interjected.

"What?" gasped Garrick.

Reynolds rubbed the bridge of his nose. He was clearly under pressure.

"I had my French counterpart yelling at me in extremely fluent English. He wanted to know why a pair of Brits were poking their official noses on his turf."

"She reached out to us regarding our investigation."

"She was on leave from that investigation. For the last two weeks she hadn't been allowed near that case since her husband was killed during the investigation."

Garrick and Fanta swapped an alarmed look.

"Detective Agon was placed on administrative leave because she was suddenly accusing everybody of a conspiracy of silence."

"I don't think she was wrong," Garrick muttered.

Reynolds considered that for a moment. "Tossing allegations about the French police force isn't going to win any of us any favours."

Fanta huffed. "Well, it's obvious somebody thinks we're onto something."

Garrick unconsciously brushed the hard drive in his inside jacket pocket. He and Fanta had decided not to mention it to the Transport officer who had interviewed them, and right now he felt it was something only he and Fanta should know about.

They were eventually given a police ride home by a uniformed officer. Garrick fell asleep on the sofa, face first, as the trauma of the last 24 hours finally took its toll.

· · ·

The sharp aroma of coffee woke Garrick, who hadn't moved position from his face plant on the sofa. He rolled to the side to see Wendy crouching, so they were eye to eye. She treated him to a warm smile and a kiss on the forehead before ruffling his hair.

"You smell how I feel," she said. I thought you might want breakfast."

The memories of the previous night flooded back for Garrick. He sat upright, alarmed to find he hadn't even taken his shoes or jacket off. He felt the hard drive Detective Agon had given him digging into his ribs. He blinked the sleep away as he saw a plastic-wrapped packet of *pain au chocolat* and a steaming cup of tea. Wendy's coffee, which had become a rare treat throughout her pregnancy, was steaming next to it. There was a pot of strawberry jam and a knife on a plate. Despite Garrick's insistence that putting jam onto a French pastry was a sin, it didn't stop Wendy from shuffling next to him onto the sofa, slicing a gash into the pain au chocolat and spooning in heaps of thick jam.

"What time is it?" said Garrick, still blinking the sleep away.

"Almost eleven."

"Ah, I should really—"

"Shhh," she said. "I saw the news and naturally assumed it was something to do with you." She caught his look. "Yeah, the incident in the Tunnel is the number one story pretty much *everywhere* at the moment." She waggled her eyebrows teasingly.

Garrick felt guilty. After all the danger he had placed himself in, when he returned from America, he had promised Wendy he would never again place himself in a life-threatening situation.

Wendy continued. "One thing I've learned is to stop worrying about these things. If you're not home and it's late, fine. It's because you're doing whatever needs to be done. I had quite a good night's sleep, to be honest."

"I'm happy my potential mortality lulls you to sleep," he said, reaching for his tea and taking a welcome sip. He noticed a pile of what he had first assumed was junk mail. He fanned five leaflets apart and noted they were all from local estate agents. "Building a collection, are we?"

Wendy grunted noncommittally as she crammed the sugar-infused breakfast into her mouth.

"It's a bit of a coincidence," he pressed, waiting for her to slowly chew the food, knowing she was deliberately doing so to annoy him and force him to make conversation. He looked around the cramped living room. A lot of space was filled with packaging, a mattress, a pram, and a child's car seat. It occupied a substantial part of the room, and he started to wonder just how much space they would have with a little one running hell for leather around. "I mean, this place is palatial," he said, avoiding her eye. "And when I say palatial, I mean, well, cosy. That's the word I was looking for. Cosy. A nice little family home."

Wendy finally found her voice again. "Cosy and little are the words. And when my mum comes it gets even cosier."

Garrick shot her a look. "What do you mean your mum comes? She's not moving in with us."

Wendy's parents didn't live too far away, but the alarm in Garrick's voice amused her. "Of course not. Well, not for more than a night or two maybe if we need help and, you know, you're working unsociable hours and causing mayhem. It is important to have a support network." She patted the couch. "Which means your days on this thing are numbered."

"Ah," said Garrick. "This is the most comfortable bed in the house."

She shot him a look. "If you carry on with that line of thought, it will be one you'll be regularly using." She made a dramatic sniff of the air and scrunched her face. "I swear pregnancy is making me smell things more. It's like a reverse Covid."

Garrick looked down at his scrubby clothes and nodded. "You know what pregnancy's also done to you, Wend?"

She raised an eyebrow.

"It's made you lose your subtlety, my dear," he said in his best Sherlock Holmes impression; an impression he had never been very good at. He knocked back the rest of the tea, which scalded his throat, kissed her on the forehead, and headed for a shower and a change of clothes. He dragged his feet; he was already dreading the day ahead.

He wasn't too surprised to find Fanta in the office with bags under her eyes and two empty cans of Red Bull on her desk. The rest of the team expressed their concern with no more than two brief sentences before reverting to business as usual. They'd long ago decided that there was no point in dwelling over the bad things that had happened. Often a knowing nod and a hot drink was more than a good enough salve to focus the mind and reassure the recipient that there was a team behind them.

The murder board had been completely rearranged, with the far right-hand section containing maps of the Pas-de-Calais region of France, and a file picture of Detective

Celine Agon. Now he was looking at it, he couldn't unsee a sadness behind her eyes, even though he knew it was in his mind. She'd lost her husband and had been suspended on leave, trying to track down the culprits, who, by the very looks of it, were embedded in her own department. And now she was missing.

Garrick had always considered himself an optimist who erred more towards reality, but in this case, he thought it was inconceivable that ruthless thugs who launched a blatant assassination attempt on British cops in the Channel Tunnel would leave this woman alive. It went against his better judgement and instincts to even think time should be spent trying to foil a potential kidnapping, when murder was the obvious conclusion.

Fanta joined him and opened another Red Bull. The can cracked with a distinctive snap. "At least she gave us a solid lead. It turns out speaking French is handy after all, eh, Guv?"

"I'll put you in for another commendation," he muttered.

It was as close to a bonding moment the two of them would ever admit to, as they turned their attention back to the board, and Detective Agon's picture.

"I found out a bit more," Fanta said. "Her husband was part of the investigation team into human trafficking and the organ harvesting. They got close to a gang, and he went in undercover. Somehow, they found out who he was and killed him. The case was immediately taken over by the French Internal Affairs. She started to get angry, understandably, and refused to take compassionate leave. She pushed the investigation, and Internal Affairs closed it all down. She was suspended on full pay," Fanta gave a side-long glance at Garrick, "which, you know, is a decent punishment for people firing guns in the middle of a train carriage. I'm just putting it out there."

Garrick nodded sombrely. "Noted."

Fanta continued, "She got frustrated, started to accuse the department of a cover-up and, of course, Internal Affairs definitely didn't want to hear that. Somehow, she managed to intercept the email Harry sent through regarding our case. It was easy for her to make sure the rest of the department didn't know what was going on and pose as the active detective in the case."

"The Super made it very clear we wouldn't have been welcome over for our investigation."

"Fancy that, sir," Fanta replied. "I guess the old Entente Cordiale is very much overlooked these days."

Garrick stared at Celine Agon's picture, his earlier thoughts about her fate resurfacing.

"Did you have a chance to look at the hard drive yet?" Fanta asked, her eyes never straying from the board.

"Nope, not yet. And I just haven't got around to admitting it as evidence, either."

"Interesting," said Fanta. "So, I was trying to work out how our photos ended up in a lovely plastic folder in the hands of two hitmen. Our warrant card photos are on a protected database. But possibly the one with the widest access, because HR can access it."

"That doesn't help us."

"No, it doesn't. But what does help us is that the hitman who wanted to play the part of a sandwich between my poor car and the van has regained consciousness." She met Garrick's eyes. "He says his name is Ameen. He's in the William Harvey Hospital."

Garrick inhaled a sharp breath. "You know what I just

remembered, Fanta? I need to go to Ashford. Have a look round the Designer Outlet Village there. Pick up some baby things. It'd be good to get a woman's advice on what to buy."

She shot him a look. "What the hell do I know about picking things for a baby?"

Garrick smiled wryly. "You really need to practice the art of reading between the lines, Detective Liu."

Chapter Sixteen

They found Ameen in the private ward of Ashford's William Harvey Hospital, protected by a young, yawning, police officer who was slouched in a chair opposite the ward, sipping her coffee and glancing at her phone when Garrick arrived. She quickly put it away when Garrick showed his warrant card. He smiled, gesturing she shouldn't put the phone away.

"I know how boring this can get," he said with a smile. "Is he talkative?" He cocked his head towards the room.

"I'm not sure," she said nervously.

Garrick and Fanta entered to find a doctor waiting for them.

"I haven't really got time to hang around here, officer," said the doctor, somewhat curtly. "There will be a nurse on standby if you need her, but he is under a lot of pain medication so I can't imagine he'll be much trouble. He seems rational enough."

Garrick waited for the doctor to leave. Ameen lay horizontally in bed. The sheet covered him up to his chest, but from the irregular shape underneath, Garrick could tell there was some gruesome support work on the man's ribcage that had gone into keeping him alive. Ameen's spinal cord had been crushed and he may never walk again.

"I'm Detective Inspector Garrick, this is Detective Constable Liu from the Kent Constabulary, but I think you know that, don't you, Ameen?"

Ameen studied him with wide eyes, although any other emotion was concealed behind a mask of desperation. Garrick pulled up a chair and sat close to his head. Liu stood next to the window. She held up her phone.

"I'm recording this interview. Time is 12:18, present DCI Garrick, DC Liu and Ameen," she said.

Garrick crossed his legs and leaned back in the uncomfortable chair. "You know more about us than our poor old mothers. Do you want to tell me how?" Garrick asked.

Ameen stared at the ceiling for a long moment. "I'm sorry," he finally said.

It wasn't quite the confession Garrick had been anticipating. From Fanta's expression, neither had she. If anything, it seemed to frustrate her. Garrick decided it best to let the man pursue his own train of thought.

The silence deepened before Ameen finally fixed his gaze on DC Fanta Liu, as if studying her Chinese heritage at a molecular level.

"I left my town in Kurdistan. My family had been persecuted for years and one by one they'd left and found a home here in your country." He paused again. "It became my dream to see them again. To be reunited with my family. So, I left. I don't know if you're aware of how long it takes to travel from Iraq to here when you don't fly and the countries do not pass beneath you," he snarled. "Travelling through the heat of Syria's deserts and the cold mountains of Turkey. Through Europe, across the Alps, mostly by foot." He tapped his legs with his balled-up fists and gave an ironic snigger. "Not that I have use for them anymore."

"Back home, I was a dentist. Fully qualified. I had good customers. It paid well. But when you leave the boundaries of your own country, your skills do not matter to others. In France, what can you do with no money, no job, no friends, no family?"

Fanta rolled her eyes and gave a sigh. She was more of a hardened cynic when it came to such sob stories. And the fact the man had tried to kill them meant she was never going to sympathise with him on any emotional level.

Ameen picked up on her thoughts. "It's easy to make judgements."

Fanta opened her mouth to comment but thought better of it when she remembered they were being recorded.

"And I mean that for myself," Ameen continued. "When you're desperate, human life is nothing. I needed the money to cross, and I was told about harvesters who could help me. But it is not cheap. How do you think any of us could afford such a thing? We're forced to fight every step of the way."

"The people I was introduced to paid well. All I had to do was sell them the parts of my body that I could do without. I was told if I sold my kidney, I would have the money to cross, to be reintroduced to my family, and maybe money to start a life. Of course, I knew the medical implications of this, and I knew I could live without it."

He paused, his gaze intensifying. "I could survive without it more than I could survive with it, stranded in a refugee camp where I could not even turn around and walk home. What would you have done?" He stared at Fanta with an accusing look. He took a moment to calm himself down.

"It's a frightening prospect and despite their assurances, I knew there could be complications. Then, to my surprise, they offered me an alternative. They wanted people to disappear. And they knew about both of you. And the French cop."

Garrick leaned forward; his interest piqued.

"Four of us were offered counterfeit documents, passports. Everything we needed to cross over without scrutiny. Without effort. Without paying a penny. Without parting with a piece of my own flesh. All we had to do was watch what you did in France. Who you spoke to. And then kill you. That was the offer. A life for a life."

He bit his lip, and tears rolled down his cheek. "I've never so much as kicked a dog in my life. I am sorry to say it was an offer that was too good to be true." His voice grew hoarse with emotion. "And you cannot understand utter desperation. When there is nowhere to turn to, you will do anything. Such deals are lifelines. I didn't know the other men, we'd never met before, but I understood we were all in the same pit. Two of them stayed behind to deal with the French woman, and we were to stop you."

He lapsed into silence, staring once again at the ceiling. This time, it went on far too long for Garrick, who needed to press him.

"So, you came up with the idea of shooting us in public?"

"We were told to try and deal with you here, not on French soil. To make your deaths spectacular. They wanted this to be a warning everybody would hear. It would make others stay away from the business."

They'd certainly achieved that, thought Garrick, making

international headlines. People were discussing terrorism, which was another convenient cover for the organ harvesters, allowing them to slip away into the shadows where they lurked.

"We were told that cameras would be disabled on the trains."

"And silenced pistols would be easy and quick," Garrick said, instantly regretting he was leading the man's statement.

"Exactly," Ameen replied. "And then we drive off. By the time anybody sees you are dead, we would be on the road and away, free, a whole new life ahead of us." He shook his head, more tears forming in his eyes.

"Your new friends failed to disable the cameras," Fanta pointed out. "Of course, that makes it look like a perfect terrorism action, and not the act of two desperate people. You were set up to take the fall. And as an act of terrorism, when you emerged at the other end, an armed response team would have dealt with you very neatly. The fact you're alive right now is pure luck." She glared at him with a cool demeanour that sent a chill through Garrick. He'd never seen his young DC so emotionally charged, and she'd had a lot of reasons in the past to feel this way.

Ameen snorted derisively. "You call this luck?" he gestured to his broken body. Killing was not something we were at ease with. A dentist and a teacher, now murderers? We debated it the moment we were on the train. We talked about not doing this, about just driving off on the other side."

"Why didn't you?" said Garrick.

"Because they know everything about my family here. They made the repercussions of failure very clear. We had no choice. Imagine if we turned up in England and tell them we have false documents, but our families are in danger.

What do you think would happen? We would be arrested, imprisoned, deported." His fists shook in anger. "And then, one day, weeks, months later, they would send us a message using our families as the victims." He swallowed hard, choking back a sob.

"The other man with you, what was his name?"

"He was from Mauritania, as far as I knew. He had been a teacher. And he had been unable to have a life either. He was a religious man. Me, not so much."

"Well, one thing I've learned," said Fanta, "is when it comes to the question of good and bad, religion is just as much in the dark as the rest of us."

Garrick studied Ameen with pity. His gaze was drawn to the man's covered legs. He now faced an equally bleak life as a paraplegic who will have the full weight of the law thrown at him."

"Can you identify the people you spoke to in France?" Garrick asked.

"We met just one man who controlled everything. He had a people. Many men. A Swiss woman, I think. There were lots of them."

Garrick reached for his phone and pulled up a picture of Dr Kabir Iyer. "Have you ever encountered this man?"

Ameen squinted. "I don't know. I don't think so."

Garrick scrolled through to another picture of the woman leaving the hospital with Dr Kabir Iyer following. "Are you sure? She'd had an operation, and I think she was a recipient of one of these donated kidneys."

Ameen peered at the picture and angled the phone with a trembling hand. "I have seen her."

Garrick felt every muscle in his body tense at the sudden

revelation. He quickly scrolled through to a clearer picture of her face.

"Yes, she's a very beautiful woman. I saw her at the camp a couple of times."

"A refugee?"

Ameen gave a dry snicker. "No. She was the snake."

Garrick and Fanta exchanged a confused look.

Ameen indicated the jug of water and licked his lips. Garrick poured a tumbler half full and moved it close to the man's lips. He had to Ameen's head forward so he could take a sip. He downed the cup in one gulp.

"By snake, you mean she was part of the operation?" Garrick prompted.

"She was the face of the operation. A siren lulling us with promises of a new life just for a pound of flesh." Ameen's voice was growing weaker. "She was always with a big man. Bald. Always dressed in black. In the finest clothes. There's no doubt in my mind that he was running everything."

Then he tapped the phone. "And this woman, this whore," he choked momentarily. "She was always by his side."

Chapter Seventeen

Only when attempting to leave the hospital did Garrick and Fanta run into a small knot of reporters hanging around the car park. News that the alleged terrorist was recuperating in the hospital had leaked. DCI Garrick had been all over the press in the last couple of years. If they saw him leave the building, suspicions would be confirmed, and there was a genuine concern that a security issue might unfold in the busy hospital.

Keeping as far back in the reception area as he could, he spotted the wavy, red-bobbed cut of Molly Meyers talking to a cameraman who had placed a TV camera on the floor between his legs as he vaped. That cinched it. The moment he and Fanta walked out the door, Molly would set upon them.

"Damn it," he muttered under his breath. "We're penned in."

"How about I cause a distraction?" said Fanta. "Set off the fire alarm, or something."

Garrick was incredulous. "In a hospital?"

Although Molly knew DCI Liu, she was confident the reporter wouldn't immediately recognise her. Plus, Fanta was dressed down in a track suit and a black padded coat with an oversized hood. She could probably easily walk by the knot of reporters without rousing suspicion. "Maybe I could bring the car right around to the door," she suggested.

"Too risky. You heard what the Super said. If we drop the ball on this, we're both in trouble."

They were in the outpatients' section of the hospital. Garrick had been here enough times to know that by cutting through several corridors, they could potentially sneak out the Accident and Emergency entrance. The only problem was, they'd still have to cross the car park to get to their vehicle.

"Okay, Fanta, you get in the car and meet me at the ambulance drop-off."

DC Liu pulled the hood of her sweatshirt up, stooped over a little, and walked out of the hospital with her hands shoved in her pockets. The few reporters who noticed, ignored her as she crossed at the zebra crossing leading into the car park.

Garrick quickly walked down familiar clinical corridors as he headed for A&E. He pushed a swing door open and entered the reception area, just as a gurney from an ambulance rushed past, surrounded by nurses and paramedics. He pressed against the wall to give them space, and caught sight of a prone middle-aged woman with blood across her face and chest, and an oxygen mask over her mouth. With the neck collar on, he guessed she'd been in a traffic accident.

As he reached towards the door, he saw the ambulance outside that had dropped off the patient was still idling with its doors open. Garrick veered to the right, cutting past the back of the ambulance intending to meet Fanta at the edge of the drop-off point, but slowed his pace, realising that she would need time to pay for parking—

Suddenly, a huge hand gripped his arm. He looked up to see a bear of a man who appeared to be kidnapping him. He tried to resist - but felt another meaty hand on his shoulder, crushing with such force Garrick winced in pain. He was about to snap his head back to break the man's nose when he spotted who was sitting in the ambulance.

She was a striking, slender woman in a dark suit, perched on the edge of a jump seat. Her long black hair was held in a ponytail, and she wore a perfectly cut black suit. She lazily smiled at Garrick as she gestured for him to enter.

"David, such a long time," she said, patting the seat beside her.

Garrick hesitated, but the grip holding him relaxed, and he stepped up into the back of the ambulance. The woman was a blast from the past, part of some unspoken Military Intelligence operation who had guided and offered vital leads on the case of John Howard, the serial killer he thought had been his friend. She hadn't done so because of any sense of justice, but because Garrick had uncovered the killer's network extended into the ranks of Government. Her sudden presence evaporated Garrick's resistance and was now feeding his curiosity.

"Ms Jackson. I'm not too sure how nice it is to see you again. But for the sake of manners, let's say it is." He sat opposite her on another folding jump seat. His beefy minder slammed the doors closed for privacy. "I'm guessing this has to do with everybody yelling about terrorists in the Eurotunnel."

She shrugged casually. "We know what it really was, don't we?"

Garrick wobbled as the ambulance pulled away. He gripped a strap on the ceiling to steady himself. "Um, where are you taking me?"

"I thought you wanted to get away from the press. Don't worry. This isn't a taxi service. I'll drop you off. I thought I'd provide a nice, quiet place to talk."

"You know, commandeering an ambulance is illegal. And they're really needed for, you know, *serious* work."

Ms Jackson smiled and shrugged. "I assure you that this is serious work. It's not as though you're going to arrest me for stealing the vehicle, is it?"

Garrick thought it wasn't the right time for a smart-arsed reply. "Okay, so what's this about?"

"Well, it's partly about France," she said, looking thoughtfully at him. "You see, our counterparts in the CNCT - *Centre National de Lutte Antiterroriste.*" She rolled her eyes at his blank look. "Or the National Counter-Terrorism Centre for those who don't remember their French from school."

"I think you and I went to very different schools."

Ignoring him, she continued. "They are aware of irregularities in the police force. Irregularities that have their fingers mostly in the Internal Affairs Department who are too eager to quell investigations when they take a wrong turn. Or rather, a correct turn, such as Detective Agon's case."

"Have they found her?"

"I don't think that's a likely outcome, judging by the people behind this. The security services there have been trying to track down the very same gang you seem to have stumbled across with your amazing combination of bluster, luck, and grisly charm."

Garrick smiled. "I should bottle it up and sell it."

"So, what have you got for me?" she mused, her green eyes twinkling at him.

Garrick pulled out his phone and showed her a picture of the woman. "Do you know who she is?" He braced himself, expecting and waiting for an answer that would push his case forward. Instead, Jackson blinked in surprise.

"She was not the focus of our investigation, I'm afraid."

Garrick put his phone away and felt a swell of disappointment. "Well, other than ferrying me out of the hospital, I don't think you've been particularly much use."

"Ouch. Is that a zing at my professional pride?" she purred. "Perhaps I have a few titbits of information from the French inquiry that affect *our* shores. That's really my area of concern."

Garrick was about to ask who when his phone bleeped, and an email arrived. A quick look at who it was from showed just a mass of random looking alphanumeric characters. His instinct was that it was spam – but he hesitated from deleting it when he saw the attachment was a photograph of a large bald man in an expensive white suit and black shirt with two large signet rings on his right hand, his left around the arm of the very woman he'd just shown a picture of.

"But her business partner is a different matter. That's Patrick O'Connell, an Irish national, who has a very nice pile in Hampstead, and appears to spend a lot of his business time down here in your neck of the woods."

"Who is he?"

"Oh, despite pleasant appearances, he's a very grungy criminal. His family ties run to the IRA, a little bit of narcotics here, a little bit of arms dealing there. He really caught his stride with a successful human trafficking operation. Cramming people in the back of lorries and not giving a damn if they suffocated or not. Naturally, he always kept himself several steps away from culpability. He was never going to be caught in the limelight of a news story. And certainly not in a police investigation." They swayed as the ambulance took a roundabout at speed. "And then he struck on the lovely world of illegally cultivating and supplying human organs. Ideally from willing donors he could pay off, and who would keep silent. It was much smarter than creating a pile of bodies to trip over."

Garrick frowned as he tried to piece together the information. "So he was in a relationship with our mystery woman?"

"We know little about her. It appears she was a French `. And I don't think it was a relationship. They ran the gang together. She was the glamour. Going to elite parties to find prospective ill businessmen or ailing dowagers. Targeting high-net worth individuals with their services. He was the brute force, bringing the donors to the table, so to speak."

"Until...?"

"Reports of trouble in paradise."

Garrick's mind reeled as he reframed the case. So far, he had placed the woman as a victim, then a cog in the machine, but now it looked as if her death may have been the result of a common source of tension: rival business partners unhappy with the direction they were taking.

"Where can I find him?"

"Oh, you'll be able to find him. But this is a man you really don't want to find. He will go to great length to protect himself. And he can afford the finest lawyers, so without incriminating evidence..."

Garrick swore as he suddenly jerked forward when the ambulance came to a stop.

"This is your stop." She gestured to the door.

"That was it?" said Garrick in confusion. "No full case file, no open leads?"

Ms Jackson shook her head. "Sorry. As much as I want this scumbag put away, there's not much I can do. I was hoping this may trigger your inner hunter."

"What's your interest in it?" asked Garrick.

"National security, of course. This is a man who transcends borders. And the moment anything in the form of terrorism that pops its ugly head up, we must eliminate it. Good luck, detective."

Garrick stepped out the back of the ambulance and found himself standing at the edge of a dual carriageway. He wasn't too sure where he was.

"Oh, detective!" Ms Jackson called. "You really would be doing me a solid if you can bring this man to justice quickly. Our French counterparts are on the verge of making arrests on the Internal Affairs stooges on their side. They've delayed, but their patience is wearing thin. When that happens, the fear is everybody over here will simply vanish like dust in the wind."

"Well, I think all you've done is taken me one step sideways. Useful, but useless at the same time."

She shrugged. "Until next time, David." She winked at him and stepped forward, closing the doors. The ambulance pulled away with its blues and twos blazing.

Garrick looked around again, hopelessly lost. Traffic rushed past him. A minute later Fanta pulled over in the pool car, with its hazard lights flashing. He hurried to join her and climbed into the passenger seat.

"What the heck happened?" she asked. "I just got some random text telling me to pick you up here."

"I just bumped into an old friend," he said thoughtfully. He held up his phone, showing her a picture of Patrick O'Connell. "We need to verify this was the same man who's turned up in the refugee camps."

"Do we have to go back to France?"

Garrick pondered that for a moment. It wasn't high on his list of things he wanted to repeat, and with the corruption simmering in their legal ranks, he feared a second assassination attempt would be successful. Then Ms Jackson's words came back.

What have you got for me?

Her tone had been teasing and playful. Her basic starting point was knowing more than Garrick did. His hand fell on the hard drive, still in his jacket pocket. He pulled it out.

"It's time we took a look at what is on this."

Chapter Eighteen

The same photograph of Patrick O'Connell that had been emailed to Garrick, now filled the screen of Fanta's laptop. The hard drive had contained folders of case files, all in French, and numerous photographs of refugees who had been forced to sell organs to pay their way.

The case files were property of the French police, which put Garrick's investigation in curious legal waters. Detective Agon had swiped them all when she had been suspended from the investigation.

She appeared not to have a name associated with the single image of Patrick O'Connell, and Garrick wondered if that was because his name had been removed by the corrupt force members that were protecting him. But what intel Agon had lacked on O'Connell was more than made up for by an image of Jane Doe accompanying him in the camp. Four more showed her talking to refugees, and in one instance, handing over a wad of banknotes.

Had Ms Jackson obtained the same images and knew

more than she'd let on? Garrick was annoyed to think she was toying with him just to further her own investigation into areas she couldn't get involved, or had she genuinely reached a dead end?

The key now was that Detective Agon had a name: Marion Fabergé.

Garrick addressed the rest of the team as Fanta put up the new information on the board.

"Patrick O'Connell and Marion Fabergé appear to have been effective business partners for at least three years. She isn't French... she's Swiss. She doesn't have any criminal record. The best we can make out is that they met at some swanky social function. Cannes, Monte Carlo, Geneva. The sort of parties you only get invited to with money. It is likely they used these venues to tout for business. But instead of showing folks a dodgy Rolex, they were offering to rebuild them."

"Like the Six Million Dollar Man," Harry quipped.

"Not far wrong, Harry. Her medical records are held in a private clinic in Geneva, so getting any help out of them is like getting blood out of a stone, but our missing colleague in France found some overlap with a clinic in Paris. Marion went there twice when she developed polycystic kidney disease. It causes cysts that lead to kidney failure."

Chib snapped her fingers. "Which is why she needed an operation!"

Garrick nodded. "And it just so happened she could get one off the shelf from her partner. What happened next with Dr Iyer and Uroš..." His fingers danced across their pictures. "We still need to work out. But it looks as if the donated kidney was rejected by her body."

He looked at his team and waited for their feedback.

Everybody was processing the new angle, but only Chib looked as if she'd chewed a wasp. "DS Okon... what have I said that pissed you off?"

She indicated between O'Connell and Marion. "They were running a strong business. If their relationship was a healthy one, then surely she'd get the operation done in a proper clinic and not in the back of Iyer's shed."

Garrick hesitated. She had a point. Chib bulldozed on.

"And then she goes to see Iyer in hospital. She's in distress. It doesn't sound like a woman relying on her husband. It sounds like one avoiding him. What if he refused to get her a new kidney?"

"That would account for her apparently being kidnapped on the boat," Wilkes pointed out. "And the clandestine stuff in picking up Uroš."

"That's an interesting line," Garrick said thoughtfully. "If he was looking for a way to get rid of her, her dying is perfect, right?"

"Pretty callous," said Harry with a low whistle, "even for a heartless bastard like our boy O'Connell. Anything on him?"

"Well, that's the thing," said Fanta, "not much on him, no criminal record, few speeding tickets. Butter wouldn't melt in his mouth."

"That's the perfect mob-boss," said Sean. "He sets everybody else up to take the fall. To earn the riches."

Garrick sighed once again, dismayed that crime paid so handsomely, delivering wonderful carefree lives for the criminals, carefree that is, right up until justice caught them. He wrung his hands together and started to pace, hoping it would kick the old brain cells into action, as it usually did.

"Marion had a replacement kidney, which was taken

from Uroš, hence the DNA confusion. He sold it to pay some debts. But rather than survive, he went missing. Paying the donors was a clean way of keeping everybody silent and leaving no bodies that could be traced." He peered at the Serbian's picture. "So, what went wrong?"

"And where's the body?" Wilkes chimed in. "And thinking about that, why make Iyer's death so public?"

Then Chib said, "the first operation went wrong. Uroš was the replacement." She caught everybody's puzzled look. "What if Iyer was being punished for incompetence?"

"The French surgery had been shut down. His was the only one left," Fanta pointed out. "How did Agon's team know about that? Maybe they thought Iyer was responsible for telling the cops?"

"Don't ignore the fact Marion's death could still have been an accident. A struggle on the boat," Chib suggested. "She goes overboard, washes up on the beach. Why go to the effort of bringing her back alive?"

"Possibly," said Garrick, "but in that case, if she's such a key influential figure, why didn't they jump in after her, fish her body out? Why carry on the boat ride and ground the boat in East Sussex? They were in a rush. To me that points to a murder. A dump and run."

A thoughtful hush settled in the room, ruined only by a clunky rattle.

Garrick moved closer to the picture of Iyer's yacht. "Patrick O'Connell and Iyer made a packet together. What if they went fishing together? Fanta, circulate O'Connell's picture to the harbourmasters in Rye and Sandwich."

"Okey-dokey." She hesitated. "Everybody said Iyer was a creature of habit, wasn't he?" She tapped the boat. "He always went to the same place to fish?"

Siren's Call

"Yeah. His boat's GPS confirmed that."

"Well, shouldn't we check it out?"

Garrick looked at her blankly. "It's the sea, Fanta. I don't think we're going to find a secret *Love Island* out there."

She looked irritated. "Why go to the same place time and time again?"

"Because he caught a lot of fish."

"And what if every trip wasn't a fishing trip?"

"Then..." Garrick trailed off.

"Then it's a terrific cover for doing other stuff," Fanta finished.

Garrick was drawn back to the map on the wall. A red dot marked the GPS location, five miles northeast of Margate. There was no reason to go out there, yet he realised Fanta had a point, and he took a moment of pride that he'd trained her to be a chip off the old block, and not to believe anything until she had seen it for herself. Of course, it was a much better thing to believe rather than the alternative, which was the awful truth that with the pressures of Wendy and recovering from the trauma he'd been through, and maybe even coming off his medications, that he was starting to overlook the most obvious things in the world.

Chapter Nineteen

The jolt almost shook the fillings from Garrick's mouth, and his grip increased to hold him steady. Fanta was looking green next to him. She leaned over the gunwale of the boat and gave another dry heave that turned his stomach.

They were on board a police launch that skipped across the waves at 45 miles per hour, following a Severn Class RNLI Royal Lifeboat, with a dark blue hull and distinctive bright orange bridge. They had launched from a port in Margate, in a rapidly assembled recce.

DC Liu's comments the day before had struck a nerve about the surgeon's fishing expeditions. So much so, that it wasn't just him and Fanta taking the trip. On the lifeboat ahead, DC Sean Wilkes had joined them. Garrick had done some diving in his time, and in his younger days had gained his PADI certificate, although it had been a while since he'd last done so. The tingling of anticipation in his stomach reminded him that diving was an old pleasure he'd long ago overlooked in favour of a darker lifestyle. On the other hand,

Siren's Call

Sean was fully qualified and still a keen enthusiast. He holidayed in the Red Sea and the Caribbean just to indulge in one of his favourite pastimes.

Garrick had expected Fanta to be an all-round expert, but she wasn't, and she was a poor swimmer.

"We're close," the police skipper at the helm indicated ahead. Garrick looked in every direction. There was nothing. No sign of land in any direction, no forgotten wartime structures like the ones off Kent's north coast. Considering they were mere miles from one of the busiest shipping lanes in the world, the lack of traffic was surprising.

The lifeboat was kitted with special sonar search equipment. As they neared the GPS coordinates of the surgeon's favoured fishing grounds, the police launch slowed to a stop and the lifeboat began to circle the area, bobbing gently in the water. They were lucky the weather was calm. The blue sky dappled by the occasional wispy grey cloud, and the gentlest of breezes that brought a north-easterly chill to the bright red survival suits Garrick and Fanta had been required to wear in case they fell overboard.

Sean Wilkes' voice crackled over the radio. "They're preparing the scan. How are you holding up, Fanta?"

She had gripped the walkie-talkie so fiercely throughout the ride that Garrick wouldn't have been surprised if she'd left cartoon finger imprints in the plastic case. She inelegantly wiped her mouth with the back of her gloved hand and shot Garrick a warning look not to betray her condition. She clicked the radio and mustered a confident voice. "No problem here, it was a fun ride," she lied.

"They're lowering the array now," said Wilkes. They watched as a rear mechanical array, that reminded Garrick of a farmer's plough, was winched into the water. A steel cable gently unwound, allowing it to extend behind the ship. They watched as the lifeboat began criss-crossing the area in a steady series of tight lanes, putting Garrick in mind once again of ploughing a field.

The Navy search-and-rescue specialist they'd recruited, had described the kit as a side-scan sonar rig, able to penetrate 20 metres down, pinging sound waves just like a dolphin. Sensors would listen for the return signal and form a 3D map of the seabed. He'd warned them that the chances of finding anything at the best of times were slim, pointing out how long it had taken them to find the Titanic, and everybody knew where that had sunk. And in this case, nobody was certain what they were looking for.

Garrick patiently leaned against the gunwale of the boat's prow, and watched, enjoying the gentle rise and fall of the police boat and revelling in the clear salty air that cleansed the cobwebs and greyness from his mind.

After an hour, he pulled out a Snickers bar from his jacket that Wendy had thoughtfully remembered to pack for him, and he offered it to Fanta. She gave a sharp shake of the head. She'd regained the colour in her cheeks but hadn't moved since kneeling on the deck, clutching the gunwale, cradled in her arms as her seasickness gradually wore off.

They had allocated three hours for the search, and even that would barely cover a fraction of the vast area around them. At one point, Wilkes radioed in to say the sonar was showing healthy fishing shoals, confirming that Dr Kabir Iyer had found a decent stretch of water. Other than that, there was complete radio silence.

Two hours and sixteen minutes into the search, watching the steady progress of the sonar scan had become tedious.

Siren's Call

Garrick glanced at his watch as Wilkes' voice crackled over the radio.

"We've found an anomaly," he said cautiously.

Garrick nodded to himself and waited for more clarification. When none came, he keyed the button. "As accurate as ever there, Wilkes. Is it your car keys? Some lost shoes? What?"

There was a long pause before Wilkes answered. "We don't know, sir. That's why it's an anomaly."

Garrick frowned. The use of the word 'sir' was an odd formality he never heard from his team, outside of sarcasm or under extreme stress.

The radio clicked again. "There is a possibility it could be from the war."

"The war?" Garrick said to Fanta with a frown. He hadn't pressed the walkie-talkie button, so Wilkes continued.

"The guys here are worried that it might be a mine, sir. It's an unusual shape stretching up from the seabed."

Garrick felt a mix of emotions. Unexploded ordnance was regularly found across Europe, and occasionally washed up on beaches around the world. During World War Two, the number of moored mines both sides had planted was astronomical, and there were still many out there. Finding one posed a potential danger that the Royal Navy would have to deal with. It also gave him a sense of thrill that came straight from the pages of the old action-adventure books he read as a kid.

"So, what's the advice?" he radioed back.

"They're sending a diver down to get a visual. I'm going to go with him, if that's alright with you."

Garrick saw the concern on Fanta's face and radioed back. "No, DC Wilkes, it's not OK that you go down there.

At least, not without me. I'm suiting up, I'm coming down with you." He looked away from Fanta's clear disappointment. This was an opportunity Garrick had no intention of overlooking.

It took another 15 minutes before the police launch repositioned alongside the lifeboat, sitting just yards apart. Garrick exchanged the colourful day-glow survival suit for a neoprene wetsuit. As he slipped on the buoyancy control vest and strapped the air tank to his back, his PADI lessons started to come back to him.

The police skipper, who was also a qualified dive master, helped secure the tank and double-checked Garrick's equipment. The final test was to put the regulator in his mouth and hit the button. A blast of cold air was forced into his mouth with a harsh hissing. The sound alone triggered his memory, and he felt himself growing excited with anticipation.

He fastened the weighted belt around his waist and sat on the gunwale to slip on his flippers. He caught the Skipper's critical eye.

"What's wrong?" Garrick asked.

The Skipper pointed to his weighted belt. "I don't think that'll be enough, mate".

Garrick patted his stomach. "I've put on quite a bit of weight since I last did this. I'm sure it's going to drag me down."

The Skipper didn't miss a beat. "That's the issue. The fat's going to make you float a lot more. I think I'm going to need to add on more weight."

Fanta snorted with laughter, enjoying the insult.

"No offence taken," growled Garrick.

Another weighted belt was added. Garrick swore the Skipper yanked the fastener tighter than he should have.

Garrick looked across at the lifeboat. Wilkes and a lifeguard were similarly dressed in scuba gear. They moved into position at the side of the boat. Wilkes gave a thumbs up. Garrick did the same. Then he watched the lifeguard and his DC topple backwards off the rail, splashing tank-first into the water. Fanta was now standing, watching with some concern at the froth of bubbles that appeared around the two divers as they slowly disappeared under the water.

The Skipper gave Garrick a thumbs up. Garrick inserted his regulator with one hand, held onto his mask with the other, and then, with an excitement he hadn't felt for a decade, he toppled backwards into the water.

He was well aware that he was probably breaking a hundred health and safety regulations that the department could throw at him. But with the threat of suspension hanging over his head, he no longer cared. Ice-cold fingers of water immediately pierced his wetsuit, and he sank beneath the water in a veil of bubbles.

It was an immediate entry into another world. His rapid breathing echoed around his skull as he fought the effects of the cold. It made him sound like Darth Vader during a race, and he was mindful to steady his breath to a slow, regular pace. The more he exerted himself, the faster he breathed, and the more oxygen he would use. He levelled off in the water and relaxed. The wetsuit was designed to soak the diver and form a layer of air underneath the neoprene that acted as a thermal shield and kept his temperature even.

He was surprised by the clarity of the water. This was the North Sea, and he'd expected a swirling fog of debris, particles, and junk. Instead, he saw that he was two metres beneath the surface, looking up through crystal clear water at the barnacled hull of the police vessel above him.

As both boats were oriented in the same direction, it was easy for him to get his bearings and spot the bright orange hull of the lifeboat not too far away, with the figures of Wilkes and the lifeguard suspended below. He pointed himself forwards and gave a series of powerful kicks to swim towards them. He was aware that he was wobbling like a drunken porpoise, but he was making good speed towards them. He tried to recall every detail of the past PADI courses, and the only resonating phrase was: 'don't worry and relax'. He tried to embrace the words as he neared the divers. Dressed identically, it was the two men's physical size that set them apart. DC Wilkes' leaner, shorter body made him look like a teenage sidekick to the bigger, well-set lifeguard.

He flashed a thumbs up towards them, and the divemaster cocked his head quizzically before Garrick remembered he was giving the wrong hand gesture; that meant he wanted to ascend. He switched to an OK sign. Wilkes and the divemaster flashed the same signal back.

Gestures were the only communication, and now Garrick regretted tuning out of the rapid catch-up he'd just had on the police boat about which signals meant what.

The divemaster made a clear gesture for them to follow him. They set off in a tight pod through the water, towards the object the sonar had detected.

Although the clarity of the sea around them was good, it faded after about 10 metres. Garrick caught the occasional hint of something moving beyond that. His immediate thought was sharks, but that was driven by an irrational fear drummed up from movies and television. The coastal waters of Britain didn't have any dangerous sharks, although there were occasional reports of one or two getting lost. Even so, if a Great White had swum by, he knew enough that the terrifying creatures were actually quite benign. More people in the UK died from dog attacks than shark attacks *worldwide*. He reminded himself these dark shapes would be shoals of fish Dr Iyer coveted.

He enjoyed the moment of weightlessness, and his body responded with alarming cracks in his joints. They popped and creaked with every kick of the foot and every slight movement from his arms as his shoulders complained about the effort. Once again, he reminded himself he had just managed to regain his health when he and Wendy started to hike. But since her pregnancy, the hiking group had become a distant memory, as had any further thoughts of fitness. It was a sad indictment of his lifestyle that the Snickers bar he'd just eaten on deck was probably the healthiest thing he'd consumed in the last couple of months.

The whole experience was delightful, even in the cold North Sea, a place he'd never had ambitions to swim in. It was almost like stepping into a new world. Rather than the bland, featureless lunar landscape he'd been expecting, there were strands of brown and green seaweed stretching up to grasp him. Some were a metre or more in length, all waving delicately in the currents. Although not as colourfully exotic as he imagined the Great Barrier Reef, they held a beauty of their own, like a sub-aquatic walk through a fantasy woodland.

He had to force himself to look away from the seabed beneath and keep one eye on the divemaster as they veered slightly aside. Three sharp kicks of the fins and Garrick corrected his course, just about keeping up with the other two. Ahead, the divemaster gave a hand gesture, a slow karate motion with an open palm, and pointed.

Just on the edge of the gloom, Garrick saw what the sonar had detected. It was a thin column rising from the seabed. He frowned as they drew closer, and the clarity began to resolve itself, like an optical illusion. It wasn't exactly as he'd imagined an old landmine should look. There was a thick chain stretching from the seabed floor. He could see the end was embedded in a lump of concrete. But there was no bulbous mine suspended at the other end.

It was a body.

In shock, he involuntarily blew out a hard stream of bubbles, and noticed Wilkes had done the same. The figure was fully clothed with both ankles tethered to a chain. The divers circled around. It was probably a man; his face was half-picked by passing fish. Garrick saw a crab scuttle across his face and disappear into the man's open jaw. His eyes had been picked clean. Yet, from his clothing, there was no mistaking the sharp suit he had been wearing.

Garrick felt a pressure on his arm. He turned. Wilkes was squeezing for attention. He turned around to see his DC gesturing diagonally to the right. There was something else in the water, a little bit too far to define.

Garrick circled around the suspended corpse to get a closer look, and then stopped in the water, fearing to get any closer. There was another body suspended from a chain, anchored to the seabed. As his eyes adjusted, his brain fought to process the information.

There was not just one other body; there were many more. The divers were surrounded by a grim, macabre forest of the dead.

Dr Kabir Iyer's fishing grounds were a burial spot.

Chapter Twenty

As the least experienced diver, Garrick was the first to return to the surface to radio in what they'd found. Wilkes and the divemaster stayed in the water for another 15 minutes before surfacing, by which time they heard the thunder of a coastguard Leonardo AW189 chopper on the horizon. The bright red and white aircraft hovered just far enough out not to create too much effect on the boats.

The police skipper tuned in the radio so they could hear the pilot.

"I can see shadows in the water!" confirmed the spotter who was craning from the chopper's open side door and peering down with binoculars.

"How many do you count?" asked the coastguard.

"I can't tell. At least 20."

Garrick and Fanta exchanged a look of shock. This was a mass sea grave, and one that was not going to be straightforward to recover. Garrick could only wonder what secrets the dead would reveal from the waters beneath them.

. . .

It was a two-day operation to clear the site. Specialist Navy divers had to be summoned along with their own forensic team, who were specialists in scouring aquatic environments. There would be little information to extract as the sea was an efficient purger of forensic data. No doubt an elegant, clean solution Dr Kabir Iyer and Patrick O'Connell had struck on to rid themselves of irritating evidence. Luckily, the grim discovery was far from the prying eyes of the press.

The bodies had been flown to a naval warehouse in the nearest naval port with facilities, which was in Portsmouth, Hampshire. In Portsmouth, multiple coroners worked on identifying the victims. Garrick suspected the shadowy hand of Ms Jackson at play, as liaising with the military was never straightforward. Yet now, it was almost effortless.

During that time, Garrick's team focused on trying to uncover more information on Patrick O'Connell and his operation, while Fanta kept in close liaison with the French team. Although they were unable to report anything of their own internal findings, the Kent team were able to provide their counterparts with some sad news. One of the first identifications the coroners had made was that of Detective Agon. She had suffered a heavy beating before her feet had been attached to a thick chain which was embedded in a concrete block. This had been thrown overboard, dragging her to a watery grave. It was one of the worst, slowest deaths Garrick could imagine. The gradual snuffing out of life. Sailors used to claim it was like going to sleep. Garrick didn't believe that. The panic one must experience as water filled your lungs. Starved of oxygen, the brain would slowly shut down. But all the while, you would be conscious of everything that was happening. It was almost impossible to give an exact time of death, although it was certain the beating had occurred within hours of Garrick last seeing her, and death had come probably that very night, while he was still deep under the Channel seabed.

The news had struck a deep emotional chord within Garrick, and for the first time in a long time, he darted into the police station bathroom to splash cold water across his face. He found himself hurling a deep grieving sob at the poor woman's death, and allowed tears of frustration and grief to roll down his cheeks. He couldn't remember the last time he'd cried. He certainly hadn't over his own sister's death, but the injustice behind this one was almost overwhelming. Worse, he knew that even if they got to the kingpin himself, her exact killers would probably never be identified, along with the army of butchers that had been incentivised to take lives to line O'Connell's pockets.

He tried to freshen himself up, but his eyes were bloodshot. He stared at his reflection in the mirror and once again wondered if his emotional fragility was a side effect of withdrawing from his medication. Throughout his professional life, he'd built up a hard shell between the bleakness of the work and the reality of everyday life. Just like doctors and nurses, there had to be a division between the light and the dark, otherwise it could drive one mad. He knew dozens of good coppers who had been unable to do this. They'd sought refuge in alcohol and drugs, and their personal lives had disintegrated, due to no fault of their own.

He splashed more water into his eyes, dried himself off with a paper towel, and walked back into the office, to be intercepted by Chib.

"Portsmouth called. They identified Uroš Božović."

Garrick sat with her at her desk, and she called up some photos the coroner had taken of the Serbian lying on an examination table. Like the victim Garrick had seen, much of his flesh had been picked off, although, oddly, mostly to one side. The other half of his face was relatively intact, allowing an easier identification.

Chib explained. "The sea is good for destroying organic evidence, but there was a particularly cold current that was also useful for slowing down decay."

"It gives with one hand, takes with the other," Garrick muttered.

Chib gave him a sidelong look. "You're getting classical there, guv."

Garrick didn't rise to the bait. The Serbian was still wearing the same clothes he'd vanished in.

"Seawater doesn't make establishing a cause of death any easier, but the coroner was willing to bet it was the same as Marion Fabergé."

"That's speculative," Garrick grumbled. While he encouraged his detectives to improvise ideas around the scantest of facts, he didn't appreciate it from the science teams who were supposed to only deal in hard facts.

Chib continued reading. "Maybe not. Look. Blue paint under his fingernails. The same as Marion."

Garrick sat up in his chair. "They were on the same boat. Why?"

Chib was growing excited as she read. "So, we've got something interesting here. He's on the same boat as Marion. He'd already donated his kidney to her, and that operation was probably done in Iyer's home theatre. Not France. So, what were they doing out at sea?"

"An execution," Garrick said as it dawned on him. "He

could have been killed during the operation. Instead, he was taken out and thrown overboard right in front of her. But they both fought. The paint under their nails indicates that. They fought their captors."

Chib ran her finger over a paragraph on the report. "He'd suffered trauma across the head." She carried on reading. "Multiple traumas. Broken fingers. Ribcage broken. He was beaten to death or near death."

Chib was puzzled. "I don't get it. They pay him to donate his kidney, and then beat him to death?"

"I know. It doesn't stack up, Chib. We're missing something."

"He was found with his phone, but no wallet."

"Taking his wallet makes sense, but why leave the phone?"

Chib read in silence - then gave a little "*ooo*" of surprise. "His phone was shoved down his underwear."

Garrick blinked in surprise. It took a moment for him to process that.

"He was trying to hide it from the people beating him up. They took his wallet, so he shoves the phone down his *kecks*." He caught Chib's eye. "Sorry, it's my inner Liverpudlian rising to the surface there. Kecks. Trousers. Even the most hardened thug will hesitate from checking that out."

"It was a Samsung Galaxy. The saltwater has damaged it, but it's been sent to our digital forensic team to see what they can extract."

Garrick leaned back in his chair. "Curiouser and curiouser," he said, trying to picture the timeline in his mind. "Somewhere there was an operation, and she was given a kidney. But it went wrong, and she needed another. This time from Uroš. But that goes wrong too. Desperate, she goes back to the surgeon. They picked up Uroš again – then we have a gap before they drive out to the marina and go out on the Argonaut. Uroš is dumped at sea..."

He trailed off and jumped to his feet.

"They swapped boats."

Chib shook her head, not quite following his line of thought.

"They take the Argonaut from Sandwich Marina – somewhere they are taken off and put onto the boat we found in East Sussex. The Argonaut returns to Rye and is scrubbed clean." The image of an old magic trick, in which a coin is hidden under three cups and the punter guesses which one, came to mind. A good magician would never allow the punter to win. "Dr Iyer returns home. Only to meet with a brutal execution of his own."

"And his laptop stolen," Chib reminded him. "Plausible, except for the actual how and why of all this happened when the woman was critically ill."

Garrick sat back down and bit his lip, gazing into the space above the computer screen. His eyes widened. "This wasn't her first transplant. If the first one was rejected?" He leaned forward in his seat as he thought about it. "That's the whole point with these organs—you have to match. If they don't match, the body can reject them, literally the immune system kicks in and identifies the new organ as an attack, just like getting a cold, and it rejects it."

Chib nodded. "Then she needed a replacement. And quick."

"And Kabir Iyer chose Uroš." They both nodded. "But that doesn't go right. Surely, he would have taken extra precautions to make sure it's a suitable match. Maybe a second operation so soon after the first is risky."

Siren's Call

"But she's dying anyway. So why not try a third."

"And if the Serbian is a match... why not take his remaining kidney. The remains of which were found on the boat with her."

Chib quickly reread Uroš's autopsy report. She highlighted a line of text. "Both kidneys were removed, which killed him."

Something still bothered Garrick. "Then why beat him up? What happened between Marion and O'Connell that led to death? They had built a successful criminal gang, so what could threaten that?" He drum-rolled his fingers across the table. "Who's got the phone?"

Chib made a quick check. "Digital Forensic Team, at Ebbsfleet. It hasn't been processed yet. They're busy."

Garrick was already on his feet and snatched his Barbour from the rack. "Don't care how busy they are. I think we'd better go along and urge them to jump the queue."

Chapter Twenty-One

Digital forensics, in Garrick's view, was a bleak department that had grown to be of vital importance in the modern fight against crime. The old-school part of him refused to acknowledge that any skill was required in clicking a mouse button and scraping whatever data was squirrelled away on a hard drive. To the public, it may be astonishing that dodgy data the user thought they had deleted, miraculously reappeared to incriminate them. Garrick had attended enough courses to be bored with the basic facts behind bits and bytes and what a computer actually did when deleting a file. Despite this, the digital forensics team were held up in some quarters as the true champions when it came to fighting crime.

Luckily, D.C. Fanta Liu was an utter nerd, and revelled in any form of geeky technology. She was more than happy to go with Garrick to the Digital Forensic Team's lab, where their Super had flexed his muscles in prioritising scanning Uroš's phone.

Even on the journey along the M2, more reports had

come in and more identifications had been made. Although most of the victims would probably never be identified as some had decomposed right down to mere skeletal remains. The majority were suspected to be immigrants, bearing the scars of missing organs and operations that had gone wrong. Others had perfectly intact bodies, with their identities unknown. The team could only speculate whether they were rivals from other criminal fraternities. Some sported finer clothing, and it could only be guessed that they were business associates who had antagonised the ruthless kingpin.

It is one of the less documented and greatest frustrations of police work that cases against villains could come to a successful conclusion, backed by solid convictions and mountains of indisputable evidence - yet still there still would be many untold stories. From the suffering of victims both guilty and innocent, the personal journeys that had taken them on the path to inevitable death. So many unanswered questions, especially in sprawling cases like this. Tragic stories that were unexplored and drowned out in the noise to get a conviction. They were often avenues in a court case that the prosecutors avoided like the plague. Countless unknown victims pocked police records across the country, and indeed the world. Their lives never to be examined.

Enyi Harris defied every one of Garrick's expectations of the geek he was about to talk to. He was muscular black guy, two inches taller than Garrick, with an American twang to his accent. He had already proudly announced his Nigerian heritage before they'd even settled down in the lab. He was easy-going and conveyed an attitude of utter charm, which irritated Garrick, who wanted to be haranguing a pasty-faced nasal geek, who'd make an easy target.

Garrick checked himself. He'd never thought of himself

as a bully, yet here he was spoiling for a fight with a weaker nerd. He needed to talk to Dr Rajasekar about his meds.

Enyi indicated a sealed box through the glass window where the phone was mounted. The case had been removed, and an array of wires were attached to the chips and circuit board beneath. Enyi drew up two stools next to his own ergonomically padded leather seat and cracked his knuckles.

"As soon as I got my marching orders to shove this up the priority list, I put it in a nitrogen-sealed atmosphere to preserve what I could, due to some corrosion to the case and some seepage that got through to the board."

"You mean, it's knackered," said Garrick plainly. "I had a phone I dropped in the toilet once. It was carnage."

Enyi flashed a beaming white smile at him. "What was carnage? What you did in the toilet or the phone?" He chuckled. "I bet that was a while ago. An old plastic Nokia or something like that. Things have moved on a bit, pops. Phones are water-resistant and quite tough. The Samsung's still pretty delicate, but a nice piece of engineering. Even a couple of weeks underwater, it held off corroding for ages. It's just started to seep. I reckon another week or so, then maybe this would've been useless."

His fingers rattled across the keyboard and darted between the mouse on the Pokémon mouse mat next to him as he navigated through layers of software. Garrick had expected screens of details. Instead, it was a series of clunky, drop-down boxes, text fields, and then black screens slowly filling up with computer code and data. It made watching paint dry an Olympic sport, and he couldn't help but stifle a yawn.

"I know, I know," said Enyi. "We can only extract data at a certain rate, and if anything's corrupt, it slows everything

Siren's Call

down. Think of it like a speed bump." He tapped various windows slowly filling with code. "We're getting SIM data here. The IMEI number and, here we go, phone log, yes, okay this is all good stuff. GPS was working too."

Despite himself, Garrick leaned into the screen to watch a series of meaningless numbers appear.

"Okay, nice," Enyi said, highlighting a line of code. "Like this, for example. This is a French carrier he hooked onto, which means he was in France. Or near France." Enyi bobbed his head indecisively. "The rest of the data might verify that, but just be aware on the south coast sometimes you can flick over to a French carrier without realising it."

Garrick knew that. He'd been in St Margaret's-at-Cliffe on the south coast and been alarmed to find himself charged with roaming fees from a French carrier as the phone had automatically switched over to their network without him knowing.

Enyi tapped another screen with a progress bar inching very slowly up. "And this one is the phone's internal storage. Got a fair bit of corruption on it. But there is data."

"Which you can extract and read?" asked Fanta.

Enyi gave a chuckle. "No. No need for that. I'm making an image of it. Like a photograph of exactly the data arrayed on there. We can look at the image without ever needing the phone again."

Garrick looked blankly at him.

Enyi maintained his charming façade, reminding Garrick of a likeable substitute teacher.

"Data's just noughts and ones. And those on their own mean nothing. Could be a photo, could be text, could be, I don't know, your nan's email address. It's only when it's laid out and interpreted with the correct programming language can we then say, yeah, that's part of a photo, that's a music file. Like digital archaeology."

"Of course it is," said Garrick, forcing a smile. "That makes you a regular Indiana Jones." He glanced at Fanta, whose eyes were scanning the screen.

Minutes of silence passed as the progress bar torturously crawled upwards. Enyi seemed to get the message and indicated with his finger. "If you want to go down to the canteen and get something to eat, I can text you when we've got something, but I think it's going to be another hour at least."

Garrick nodded and offered to treat Fanta to lunch. They both opted to take a rather prosaic plate of chips and beans and sat at a table in the corner of the busy cafeteria as more people came in, some in uniform, others in plainclothes, indicating that shifts were changing. It was the first time he and Fanta had been able to have time alone since the incident in the Channel Tunnel. Her normal, chatty persona was notably absent as she picked at her food.

"How are you feeling?" Garrick tapped the side of his head. "I mean up here. It's been a rough few days."

"I'm worried about what happened on the train," she said bluntly.

"It was stupid, and you should have known better." Garrick sighed. "And you probably saved my life. And maybe others too." That got a smile from her. "The problem is the word *probably*. It didn't happen. When we make these judgement calls, it's on our shoulders if we think there is a genuine risk. Imagine if he'd shot a member of the public. We'd be in trouble for not stopping him.

"So I'm screwed either way."

"You know the game, Fanta. Rules are rules. Rules get broken. Broken rules get punished. But just sometimes, the punishment has to be a little lenient because it was the right thing to do. I'd argue your shot made him run. He could have stood there, shot me and God knows how many other innocent people."

They met each other's gaze, both recalling how terrified the assailant had been to flee and shoot himself in the head rather than face the consequences of his paymasters or being returned to his home country.

"There's no point in dwelling on it. The future's unpredictable," Garrick continued, "we'll never know, but it's a strong case when it comes to the inevitable disciplinary."

"And then my career's over." Her voice was low and cracked.

"Your track record? I don't think it's possible to end *your* career. Look at me." She arched an eyebrow. "OK, maybe I'm a bad role model. Think of this as a black eye in the fight that's your career."

She licked her lips and put her fork down. "I didn't get that promotion."

Garrick nodded. He was relieved, but thought it wasn't the best time to demonstrate that.

"I've a friend of a friend over in Manchester who reckons it's because of what happened."

"Ah, they don't want a troublemaker in their squad, eh?"

"It appears they want people who are quiet, follow the rules, keep their nose down... and don't go discharging firearms in public when they're not supposed to." She gave a shrug. "Morons."

Garrick nodded. "Total morons. If it makes you feel any better, you would have hated it there. And remember, after what happened, you should be suspended. But the Super is still keeping you operational."

Fanta scowled. "Only because we're understaffed, under-resourced, and in the middle of an alleged terrorism case. It's not going to look good," she did air quotes with her fingers, "cutting back the staff, is it? But when it's over, I know they'll want scapegoats"

Garrick always considered himself a good, or at least *adequate*, team manager. He'd strived to develop a laid-back atmosphere that was supported by rigorous attention to detail and eagerness to see justice done. Yet, he still found talking about other people's personal emotions difficult. Over the years, he had to sit by Harry's hospital bed wondering if his friend would be able to walk again. He'd sat by Fanta's side after she'd been caught in a booby-trapped explosion. He'd endured emotionally charged conversations with Chib when the duplicitous nature of her role on his team and the London Met investigation was revealed. He'd talked to Sean Wilkes, who'd started dating Fanta, and told this eager, smart, young man that his colleague and girlfriend was on the verge of death during the line of duty.

And yet now he found himself at a weird confluence of being relieved Fanta was not moving anywhere and the realisation that one way or another she would be going elsewhere. If they triggered any more controversy, his team would be disbanded despite their track record. Because those above him always needed to save face more than solve crime.

Fanta only ate half her lunch, but Garrick found himself so ravenous he went back for a dessert and risked the apple pie and custard, which he couldn't recall having for decades. The conversation remained stilted, although not awkward and uncomfortable. That was one saving grace from their closeness.

When Fanta received a text message, it had taken close to

90 minutes for Enyi to summon them back to his den. He was drinking from a can of Dr Pepper and clapped his hands together, rubbing them vigorously when they entered.

"Did you recover any emails, anything useful like that?" said Garrick.

"There's a few, but I think you'd be more interested in Telegram."

Telegram was a secure messaging app that thwarted security services and police forces around the globe due to its high levels of end-to-end encryption. Although it was used legally, it was also utilised by warring countries and criminal masterminds. It was almost impossible to hack, unless you had access to it.

"By luck, he'd already logged in, so it was an open door for me to push. What do you want to look at first?"

"Any pictures."

Enyi double-clicked a folder, and a selection of selfies and general mundane-looking pictures appeared, showcasing Uroš's life at university, hanging with friends at a Chelsea match, and the occasional amusing thing he'd spotted while out and about on the streets. After a short scroll through, Garrick and Fanta both shouted "Stop!" at the same time.

There was a photograph of Marion Fabergé. It was difficult to see where it was taken, but she glanced at the camera with a slight smile.

"Oh my God," Garrick uttered. "Why was he meeting her? I don't think it's common practice for a recipient and a donor to meet, is it?"

They scrolled through more photos taken at different times, one in a restaurant, and then stopped at a selfie of Marion and Uroš, smiling into the camera, their cheeks pushed together to get into frame. This was not two strangers meeting one another.

"Do we have metadata for the dates for these?" Garrick asked.

Enyi indicated another window. "Meta's all here. GPS location where it was taken, date."

"Two weeks before he went missing," Fanta noted.

"Where is this location?" Garrick asked, tapping a line of coordinates.

Enyi called up a map and cut and pasted the GPS coordinates into it. "London. There's a few from all over. Hyde Park. Leicester Square. Covent Garden."

Garrick tried to recall the case notes. "These dates are before the first operation. They were obviously quite close then."

They scrolled through more images of them in a pub and in a bar. With each turn of image, their body language was getting suggestively closer. Garrick leaned back in his chair to imagine the hidden life taking place behind the images of pixels.

"Maybe she was trying to woo him into surrendering his kidney?"

"Look at them," said Fanta. "These are two people very much in love, or at least good at faking it."

"Sure, but they're two different pools, right? Engineering, immigration... she was going to Monte Carlo and convincing the rich and shameless that she could fix them up for a price." Garrick rubbed his throbbing temple. "All this time we've been looking at him as a victim."

"I think all the evidence still points that way," said Fanta. "It doesn't matter if they met and fell in love."

"What was he studying?"

"Engineering and Architecture."

"Did he specialise in anything?" She looked at him blankly. "Remember his house, there were medical books there." She nodded. "What was it Forensics said about the surgeon's theatre?"

"That they were difficult to build. Celine said that too." She was picking up his train of thought. "Uroš was the guy who designed and built the surgical theatres."

"Well, what if..." Garrick trailed away. There were pieces of information missing, but he sensed they were on the right path. "She is ill and needed a transplant. Lucky for her, that's what they do. O'Connell sets her up with a replacement – but it's rejected. If they get another donor that's non-compatible, then she could die. But he is compatible. And here he is, a man in love, ready to make a very dramatic sacrifice and make the donation himself."

Fanta nodded. "Okay, I can buy into that. Why kill him?"

Enyi coughed. "Like I said, Telegram's what you need. Check the messages out."

He slid the mouse to Fanta. She scrolled through the secure communications between two lovers. Marion increasingly resented being with Patrick O'Connell and felt she was doing all the work, while he took all the money. Their business partnership was fracturing. Over two months a picture emerged that once she was diagnosed with kidney failure, O'Connell blocked her from finding a suitable donor. She became convinced he wanted to see her die a natural, quick death that couldn't draw attention to him and his operation.

Marion convinced Dr Iyer to find a donor and perform the operation in France. Already she was plotting to overthrow O'Connell and take the gang for herself. But when the operating theatre on the French farm was busted, she suspected O'Connell's hand behind it, puppeteering the French authorities he had under his control. It forced her to return home without completing the necessary recovery phase.

And that's when the second replacement went wrong, and she reached out to Iyer again. However, the plan was not to hack Uroš's remaining kidney from his body. They would find another, and in doing so, complete a coup d'état and bring down O'Connell's business by denying him the raw materials he needed. Marion and Uroš were setting their own rival harvesting operation and had convinced Dr Iyer to join them. Their plan had been for the three of them to travel to a clinic in Switzerland so Iyer could perform the operation.

They never made it there alive.

"It's like a sick version of Romeo and Juliet," Fanta commented. "Except they hack everybody else apart rather than die at the end."

"Have you ever read Shakespeare?" Garrick asked with enough incredulity to appear he had; when all he'd really done was watch a few films which he'd found boring.

"More like West Side Story," Enyi interjected. He held up his hand defensively when the detectives threw him a look. "It's all about turf wars."

Garrick didn't want to admit that the geek had hit the nail on the head. Marion had broken the heart of a merciless gang boss, but rather than play the role of innocent victim, she was ruthlessly orchestrating taking over the operation. She, Uroš and Iyer were only victims of their own amoral crimes.

They scrolled through more pictures, this time discovering images of Marion in a tight, revealing dress as she posed flirtatiously for the camera in a large, elegant white living room.

"Where was this taken?" Garrick asked.

Enyi cut and pasted the data into a map, and it came up with an address in Hampstead. Scrolling through more photos that hinted at France.

"You said there was GPS data," prompted Garrick.

Enyi grew excited and bounced a little in his chair. "Let me fire up something I've been working on. Not an official piece of software, but y'know, it's always nice to experiment. Let's see what we can see."

After a few mouse clicks, he loaded up the GPS data. The software threw up yet another progress bar, although this one took just over two minutes before it yielded a result.

"Ta-da!" he exclaimed, pointing to a random scattering of dots laid out across the screen.

"If this has joined the dots, I'm really not amused," said Garrick.

"Oh!" When Enyi clicked the mouse button, the black background was immediately replaced by a map. "Bit of a bug there. This is a historic map of his movements."

"Can we narrow down by date? Just the last three weeks," Garrick requested.

"Easy." Three mouse clicks later, many of the dots vanished.

Garrick indicated a specific area around Gravesend. "Let's start there."

Fanta leaned in and took the mouse from Enyi's hand. "This is the night he was picked up. They travel to Iyer's house for several hours, then to Sandwich Marina. Then out to France."

Enyi indicated the screen. This all tallies with the phone carrier data. You see here where it switches between O2 in the UK and Orange in France.

Fanta scrolled through the map, to the next GPS point. "The next one is at a small fishing port south of Calais. Étaples."

"They're not there for long," Enyi pointed to the timestamp. "Look, five minutes and he's heading back out. That was the last GPS log."

"That's where they changed boats," said Garrick as the facts neatly aligned in his head. "I bet some of O'Connell's thugs were waiting for them. They load Marion and Uroš up onto the other boat, and dump him in the fishing ground. Not before they scooped out the rest of his kidney. Maybe in case O'Connell was intending to help her after all. Or maybe she was just such an ice queen she asked them to do it as he was about to die anyway."

"And Iyer returns home on the Argonaut. Maybe claiming he was coerced into going with them. He thinks he's got away scot-free. Until he arrives home."

"O'Connell thinks he's left no stone unturned."

Garrick's mind was racing. He scrolled through the photos, inserting the photo of the white dress and the Hampstead house. He darted back to the GPS data and scrolled in. There it was - the same match.

"Uroš and Marion had been together the week before they made a break for it. They were in London. I bet this is where she lived."

"You know what I've always wanted to do, guv?" Fanta said as a genuine smile crossed her face. "I've always wanted to do a stakeout!"

Chapter Twenty-Two

Surveillance was an art form. While David Garrick and the team had had plenty of opportunities to sit outside a suspect's house and watch them, it was never a particularly easy job. An average suburban street with regular traffic coming and going provided easy cover. However, this address came with problems. It was a large semi-detached house behind a private gate presented unique challenges. The neighbourhood was exceptionally quiet, and so expensive, they had their own communal private security that patrolled the estate, on the lookout for any ne'er-do-wells, such as Garrick and his merry band of police officers.

In addition, this was out of the operational bounds of Kent Police, which meant they had to get swift cooperation from the Metropolitan Police. Fortunately, Garrick's track record was well regarded in the service, and the MET's DCI Kane was on hand to make sure he met no resistance.

The house itself lay at the end of a curving tarmac drive, the view blocked by a bank of large, cultivated conifer trees.

The iron gate was the sole access point and had a camera entry phone, so there was no chance of getting close.

As Garrick and Fanta sat in the seat of a borrowed BMW —a gleaming black model they hoped wouldn't stand out in this elite neighbourhood—they watched a private Crown security van slowly drive past, ignoring them as instructed as it made its usual tour of duty.

In a parallel road, circling around the back of the house, Chib and Harry Lord sat in another car. The house's garden backed onto the neighbours in this street, so there was no way the detectives could see into the target's garden. They just had to sit tight in the unlikely case somebody decided to make a run for it via the garden. They were all supported two blocks away by Sean Wilkes, who was hunkered down with SCO19 – London's Specialist Firearms Command.

Because of O'Connell's reputation and the brutal nature of his gang, surveillance could easily tilt into direct action. It wasn't a scenario Garrick wanted played out, but as the officer in charge, he couldn't take any risks.

From what they'd seen on Google Maps, the house was a beautiful white stone affair with a massive swimming pool in the manicured back garden. It was registered to a private company, which in turn was a shell company of another entity. The true ownership would be lost in layers of shifting companies designed to keep the identity of the owner away from prying eyes. Celebrities used it, as well as Russian oligarchs and criminals. The listed price of the house was £17 million, which once again had made Garrick's stomach turn, as it was undoubtedly bought on the proceeds of human suffering.

They'd been there since 5 pm, and so far, had seen no

signs of life. Fanta had argued that they should just walk up to the entrance and buzz the gate.

"We could be looking at an empty house," said Garrick.

"We don't know if she had any family," Fanta commented. "I very much doubt she lived in this place on her own."

"If she didn't, why have none of the staff reported her missing?" Garrick silently answered that for himself: they probably didn't fancy seeing themselves drowned in the North Sea for breaking their silence.

After an hour, they were both becoming restless, and Garrick reluctantly authorised the use of Harry's drone. When he'd first bought it, Harry had adopted the swagger of Tom Cruise's character Maverick from the film "Top Gun", and had bored anybody who would listen as he extolled the joys of the emerging e-sport. At the very least, it meant he'd been buying his own drones and was apparently an adept pilot, and Garrick felt it was as good an excuse as any to give him a taste of fieldwork he was craving.

Garrick sent a quick WhatsApp message to Harry: "Deploy the drone!"

They had argued about using it. Garrick thought the drone's high-pitched buzz would draw unwelcome attention in the quiet housing estate. Harry had claimed that if he kept high enough, nobody would pay attention, and the camera would give them good optics across the grounds.

Before long, Garrick started to receive photos forwarded from the drone to Harry's phone, then on to the team. Daylight was beginning to fade, but the 4K resolution of the images was something to behold. Harry had kept the camera at an angle to the property rather than flying it overhead, and had captured exactly what they needed: evidence that *somebody* was home.

There were three people in the garden, relaxing back in recliners with cans of beer and a bloodstained laptop open on the table as they talked.

"And who are you guys?" Garrick muttered to himself.

Fanta was already using her fingers to zoom in on the image as she scrutinised it. She quickly messaged Chib, telling them they needed a better angle of the faces. There was no reply, but less than a minute later, more pictures came in, offering better angles of the three men. Fanta gave a gasp.

"Oh my God! It's Patrick O'Connell." She held up the phone so Garrick could see, but he'd already opened the same photo.

"This is his house, and she lived here." They exchanged a look. "She wasn't working for him." Garrick tapped the picture of Patrick O'Connell. "This was her old man. They were in a relationship."

"Poor old Uroš," said Fanta. "That's why he was killed."

Garrick nodded as blocks of evidence fell into place like a game of Tetris, forming a strong supporting base for the entire case. Marion and Patrick had been at the heart of the operation. Not just business associates, but lovers running a notoriously ruthless gang. Ruthless people fall in and out of love. For whatever reason, Marion had engaged in an affair with Uroš. One that was exposed as she fell ill, drawing the unwelcome attention of her hardened criminal partner.

They were two ruthless people, brought down by very human emotions, and everybody else in their way was just collateral damage. Garrick corrected himself—O'Connell had not been brought down just yet. He was the devil in the background, the demon in the detail. The untouchable evil. And in killing Marion and her lover, and the surgeon, he had broken his own rules regarding not leaving a trail of bodies, and unwittingly created a pathway to himself.

Garrick was so engrossed as he stitched the various threads together that he almost didn't hear Fanta swear loudly.

"So much for Top Gun," she said sarcastically. Garrick looked at her, and she held up her phone. It seemed Harry Lord had a slightly inflated opinion of his own flying skills. The buzzing drone had drawn the attention of the criminals. They were now staring straight towards the camera.

Garrick felt his blood run cold as the next series of images came in.

The three men in the garden had disappeared.

"What do we do?" Fanta said in a tense voice.

Garrick felt cold beads of sweat form on his brow. He had no idea. They'd just cornered one of the deadliest men in the country, and without due cause, they couldn't storm the building and arrest him. O'Connell would be out of the holding cell before Garrick had time to turn the key.

"Guv?" Chib's voice crackled across the radio. She was thinking the very same question.

David Garrick had been through a lot in his career and was proud to say he had never been at the mercy of a panic attack. Yet now, he could feel the signs. A clawing in his stomach, his breathing elevating, a slight tremor to his hand. *Side effects from his lack of meds,* he told himself. Not that it helped.

He had to do something.

He opened the car door. Fanta exploded in panic.

"What are you doing?"

"Stay here. Be ready for anything."

Garrick slammed the door shut, cutting off Fanta's protests. He straightened the hem of his Barbour and walked towards the gate. He bunched his fists to stop his hands trembling. His eyes focused on the gate's security camera. It was almost as if he could feel Patrick O'Connell's gaze boring into him from the other side.

He pressed the intercom button.

"Patrick O'Connell, it's the police. We'd like to ask you a few questions about Marion Fabergé."

He released the button and waited, never taking his eyes from the camera and hoping he looked more confident than he felt. His phone vibrated in his pocket. He'd put it on silence at the start of the stakeout and hadn't checked since. The buzz indicated it was a text message. And the only person who would message him was Wendy.

Garrick turned to return to the car – when a metallic clunk from the gate indicated it had unlocked. With a faint hum, the gates silently swung open. Garrick felt like a rabbit caught in headlights. He couldn't walk away, and a step forward would be walking into a trap.

His heart hammered in his chest. He had no choice. Mustering all his courage, he walked through the gates. He fished his mobile from his pocket and glanced at the screen. It was a message from Wendy.

She had gone into labour.

Chapter Twenty-Three

The tarmacked drive curved around the trees, and Garrick quickly lost sight of the gate, although he heard it close behind him. A few yards later, he rounded the curve and saw the house. A Ferrari and black Audi Q5 were parked outside. The front garden was beautifully manicured and looked more like a pleasant stately home rather than a den of unscrupulous evil.

His fingers tightened around his phone. It took every fibre in his being to stop replying to Wendy's text message. He should be speeding home to be with her, but that option had been stripped from him.

His ears were now filled with the sound of his own heartbeat as he neared the front door. It was an intimidating piece of solid black wood, some eight feet high. It would look at home in a castle, never mind a house in Hampstead. He strained to listen for any sign that his team was following him. There was nothing. He felt totally alone.

Just a few steps before he reached the porch, the front door silently opened. It looked dark inside; he saw no signs of life. It was an invite he couldn't ignore. Slipping his phone back into his pocket, David Garrick entered the home of the ruthless organ harvester.

The circular white marble entrance hall had three doorways leading from it, and a stairway embracing the wall as it spiralled upward. All the curtains had been closed, plunging the hall into shadows. The door closed behind him with a deep thud. Garrick stopped in the middle of the room before he looked behind. One of the men who had been in the garden was on door duty. He was a massive Latino who must spend all his free time bench pressing. He was bald, with a stubby grey goatee poking from his chin. His trunk-like arms were covered in Maori inspired tattoos and his t-shirt barely fitted. The effect was spoiled by the fact he was wearing a Taylor Swift tour t-shirt.

"Mr Garrick."

Garrick turned back to see Patrick O'Connell hurrying down the stairs.

Garrick's mouth was dry as he spoke. "Mr O'Connell. I appreciate you volunteering to answer a few questions."

O'Connell was almost as big as the doorman. He wore a black shirt that was untucked over jeans. A pair of expensive-looking trainers. He stood almost nose-to-nose with Garrick, his piercing eyes looking as dead as a shark's.

"When it comes to that bitch, I don't think I have a choice." His Irish accent was smooth and melodious, at odds with his ruthless soul. "But I don't think there is anything you can tell me about her that I don't know. Like your good self, detective."

The threat lingered in the air. Garrick was aware predators like this seized on any signs of weakness. Garrick forced a smile.

"And here I was hoping we'd get to know each other a little better. She was your partner, correct?"

"We had a thing for a while." O'Connell was becoming restless. He kept glancing over Garrick's shoulder at the doorman, who was on his phone.

"I didn't catch your friend's name," said Garrick.

O'Connell sniffed and wiped his nose with the back of his hand. Garrick had seen enough coke-heads to know what was driving this man.

"Oh, he likes to be an enigma. You can call him Tom. He responds to anything." He laughed and clapped Garrick on the shoulder. "You're a ballsy man, David. I like that. I really do. God love ya, for walking in here for a natter. What, with all them drones circling the place. It's like summer. Must be attracted to all that beer in the garden."

Garrick extended both hands in a 'guilty' gesture. There was no point in denying anything.

"You're an amazingly difficult man to get in touch with."

"Well, that depends, doesn't it? As a rule, I like to be the person who *gets* in touch. I'm very picky about the company I keep."

"Like Dr Iyer?"

O'Connell tilted his head back so that he was almost looking at Garrick from down his nose.

"You know, I was just thinking about him. How is he?"

"Not doing too well."

"Oh, that's sad. Last I heard, he was running away with Marion to launch a little business of their own." O'Connell giggled and sniffed again. "I think they'd had enough of me."

"Some people don't know how lucky they are." Garrick

met O'Connell's unblinking gaze. He was getting more pissed off by the man's arrogance with every syllable. "In fact, I was just thinking, Tom over there might know a little more about the good doctor. He looks the sort."

O'Connell nodded and flicked a look at Tom. "He's a very capable man, is Tom. I wouldn't put it past him."

"You're a man who likes to keep his hands clean."

"Personal hygiene is important, Detective. It can make all the difference between life and death."

"I appreciate your candidness, Mr O'Connell. Then I suppose you won't have any objection to telling me what you know about Marion's murder."

For a moment, O'Connell looked ready to deny he knew she was dead. Then he smirked and pointed an accusing finger at Garrick.

"Ah! You thought I was about to spill me guts, didn't ya?"

"Why not? You spill everybody else's."

O'Connell physically flinched. He sniffed and wiped his nose again, and Garrick knew he'd caught him off-balance. The thug was the sort who never experienced backchat. Like most bullies, he expected to always get his way. Resistance was almost unheard of unless you wanted to be chained to a rock and tossed into the North Sea. O'Connell stepped back to reappraise Garrick.

"Like I said. Ballsy. You chose the wrong career path. You would have been bloody successful on the other side of the line."

"Lately, I've been thinking that myself. Out of curiosity, how much do you make?"

O'Connell leaned in so close, Garrick could smell the beer on his breath. He whispered into his ear.

"A feckin' lot. You should see my big house." He pulled

away, then gestured to the space around them. "But in case we have ears buzzing around, let me give you the best piece of business advice I've ever received. Deny everything, then attack, attack, attack." He glanced at Tom with a look of relief. "Ah. He's ready." He slipped his arm around Garrick's shoulder and steered him around to the front door, and began walking, like a pair of buddies catching up. "As much as I'd love to show you around and answer your questions about my entrepreneurial spirit, I think we just won't have time."

Tom opened the front door, and Garrick saw he was holding a laptop covered in dried blood. O'Connell firmly led Garrick back outside.

"I haven't asked you everything I need to," said Garrick, blinking in the sunlight. "Unless you want to answer them in the comfort of the station?"

"Tell you what, how about the comfort of my car?" He gestured to the black Audi, which had been repositioned so that it now faced the gate. The engine was running, and the third man from the garden climbed from the driver's seat and opened the back side door.

Garrick stopped in his tracks. "I don't think so."

O'Connell firmly pushed him forward. "You don't want to be turning down me hospitality now, do ya? I thought you had a lot of questions?"

Tom tossed the laptop onto the passenger seat, then reappeared with a sawn-off shotgun, which he held casually with one hand. The driver looked nervously at the sky. O'Connell shoved Garrick towards the rear driver's side door.

"Get in. Then you can ask me anything."

Garrick felt a wave of icy calm wash over him. He took one look at the shotgun, then climbed in the back of the car. The driver slammed it shut before getting back behind the wheel. O'Connell joined Garrick from the opposite side, while Tom took the passenger seat, his eyes nervously scanning the sky.

They accelerated down the drive at speed. It was perfectly timed, so they passed through the gate as it opened. The driver didn't ease off the pedal. Rubber screeched as they sped along the private street. Garrick noticed that Fanta's car had gone, but was careful not to make any obvious movements to give the game away.

O'Connell sniffed and picked at his nose. "So, what shall we talk about?"

A knot in Garrick's stomach tightened as his phone buzzed in his pocket again. He hoped Wendy was OK and taking her own advice about not worrying when he didn't answer. He desperately tried to recall everything he'd learned from yoga to calm himself. He couldn't afford to panic. Being kidnapped was a new experience for him. And wasn't he always telling people they needed to embrace new experiences?

Chapter Twenty-Four

Hampstead was an affluent area in north London but, critically, still well within the sprawling metropolis. That meant getting out of the city with any sense of haste was practically impossible. The busy, narrow streets were restrictive; a prison system for cars, and O'Connell and his men were more than aware of this.

In the back of the Audi, Garrick remained calm as the general anxiety levels rose. Patrick O'Connell was becoming more agitated as he shifted in his seat to look out of every window. He was sniffing almost uncontrollably now as the effect of the drugs kicked in, potentially making him more volatile than usual. He nudged Garrick in the arm.

"You relax, mate. You're safe with us. You're our ticket out of here."

"Do you really think they care about one lone detective when it comes to a car full of armed organ harvesters cruising around London?"

O'Connell sighed. "Jeez. Has anybody ever told you that you're such a feckin' pessimist? I'm not a killer. Not when you can make more money with a simple business transaction and not leave any mess behind."

"That's my job," Tom growled from the front, throwing a venomous look at Garrick. They bounced over a speed bump that frequented almost every road around them – and Garrick winced as the shotgun in Tom's hand wobbled dangerously. All it would take was a deep pothole and he could accidently blow Garrick's head off.

"You trade on misery, Patrick."

O'Connell was affronted. "I give people hope. I give them the chance to keep living. That's not the definition of a bad guy. People get paid to be donors. People pay for something that can cure them of whatever ails them. Where's the harm?"

"I suppose the harm is when people get in your way. Like Marion, and Uroš."

O'Connell's face screwed up with anger. Garrick had hit a nerve. "The Serb bastard. I paid his way through uni. I was giving him a head start in life – then he decides to screw me girl behind me back. I don't do betrayal, David. It leaves a bad taste in the mouth."

"You killed him." Garrick directed his hunch at Tom.

"He wanted to donate to Marion," growled Tom. "I was just helping him out."

O'Connell's voice softened. "You see, you've got us all wrong. Health care is broken around the world. People are turning to private solutions, and even then, they're bound by the most basic of all business practices. Supply and demand."

"And when Marion demanded to leave you, you cut off her supply. You'd rather she died than leave you."

"She had her shot and the transplant was rejected." O'Connell sniffed and smiled. "Turns out it had feckin'

Siren's Call

better judgement than me. That's when I found out about Uroš. But, y'know, even that could be fixed. What couldn't be fixed was her ambition to kick me down and run everything her own. I couldn't be having that now, could I?"

"Taking out the French detective was a mistake."

"She got too close. Like you."

"Well, killing me didn't go so well."

"Don't take it personally, David." O'Connell shook his head. "That's what you get for sending amateurs to do a professional's job." He stooped in his seat to get a look at the sky above them.

"Looking for something?" Garrick asked as casually as he could.

"Seeing if your little airshow is following us."

"Pat!" The driver slowed down and pointed ahead. A lorry and its trailer were blocking the end of the street.

"Take this left," O'Connell said. For the first time, he sounded nervous.

They jolted as they took a speed bump.

"There's only one way this can go, *Pat*," Garrick said, playing to the Irishman's ego. "Personally, I'm crapping myself about it because I hear you have the best lawyers on speed dial. You've been three steps ahead the whole time. Guess I got lucky today."

O'Connell shot him a hard look. It was as if Garrick could read his mind: what did they have on him?

The driver slammed on the brakes. "Shit."

The road ahead was blocked by an Amazon delivery truck parked sideways. There was no way around it.

"Take this right," O'Connell said with increasing unease.

Inwardly, Garrick smiled. He could see the net of authority closing in around them. So far, there had been no hint of police activity, yet they were being herded away from the civilian streets – and Garrick had a good idea where they were heading. All he had to do was keep the thugs unbalanced. He indicated the bloodstained laptop Tom had wedged on the centre console.

"If I were you, I wouldn't ride around with that. You're setting yourselves up."

Tom glowered at him. The shotgun waved precariously as they took another speed bump. Garrick pressed on. "Iyer's laptop. He recorded every donor and every recipient. Dangerous." He saw a rubbish skip on the road ahead and improvised. "I'd toss it in the skip if I were you."

He knew they wouldn't do something so ridiculous, but his guess as to why Dr Iyer's laptop had been retrieved had been correct. It heaped further paranoia onto O'Connell's eroding self-confidence.

"Another one!" the driver said, distracting O'Connell from the laptop. Ahead, another truck had blocked their path. The driver didn't wait for instructions; he took a right so sharply that the side of the Audi scraped a bollard, creating a long screech. "Where the hell are we going?"

"Get us out of here!" O'Connell growled.

"I can't!"

Garrick's phone suddenly buzzed. This time O'Connell heard it. His hand shot into Garrick's pocket and pulled it out.

"This the cavalry coming to your rescue?"

"I doubt it."

O'Connell read the message. An amused smile appeared on his face.

"Wendy? She's your old lady, isn't she? Giving birth a bit prematurely. Nasty."

Siren's Call

Garrick reached for the phone, but O'Connell pulled it out of reach.

"Now, now, David. I thought we were playing nice."

Cursing from the driver drew their attention outside. A tow truck was blocking their way. They took another sharp side road – and as they rounded a bend, they saw trees and an tree filled field of grass ahead. O'Connell gesticulated wildly.

"Go through there! Get us out of this shit!"

"Are you serious?" the driver whined, slowing down.

O'Connell slapped him on the side of the head. "Just do it!"

"OK! OK!" He hit the accelerator, and the large 4x4 briefly took air as they jolted onto the grass and sped forward. The park was strangely empty for an evening in London. Another message flashed on Garrick's phone. O'Connell angled the screen so he couldn't see. He sucked in a breath.

"Oh... complications." He gave a mocking look of concern. "Oh, David. I'm so sorry."

Garrick didn't think. A raw animal instinct exploded inside him, and he lunged for O'Connell. The smug boss hadn't been expecting the brazen move. Garrick repeatedly slammed the man's head against the side window with such force that he saw blood on the glass. O'Connell dropped the phone – and at the same time, Tom angled in his seat to intervene.

"COPS!" yelled the driver.

Two police cars sped from behind the trees, lights and sirens blazing. At the same time, four drones lowered from the sky and buzzed in front of the windscreen, hampering the view.

Tom switched from trying to help O'Connell, to

lowering his window so he could aim the shotgun at the police car pulling alongside. The report from the weapon was deafening inside the Audi, and the hot cartridge case bounded out at speed, bouncing around the cabin. The police car's windshield turned white as a hole was punched through it, and it skidded to a halt.

Garrick tried to lunge for Tom to stop him from firing again – but a seat belt suddenly looped around his throat, and he was pulled back by O'Connell, who was now intent on choking him to death.

A drone abruptly made a kamikaze plunge straight at Tom.

Garrick's vision began to dim as he fought to breathe, but O'Connell had him in a perfect embrace. There was no room to move in the confines of the car. He saw his phone in the rear footwell as it lit up with another message from Wendy.

At the same time, the drone struck Tom's hands. The whirling rotors severed two fingers and, as the drone ricocheted into Tom's face, he pulled the shotgun back into the car, the shortened barrel flipping over his shoulder.

Garrick's peripheral vision began to shrink, as if he was looking down into some sort of carton rabbit hole. His face burned from exertion, and the world slowed to a crawl. The driver was still going hell for leather across the park. They crested a rise – and Garrick knew where they were. Hampstead Heath. Ahead was the iconic view of London's financial centre, with skyscrapers stretching to the clouds. It was also a steep hill down.

As Tom's shotgun completed its arc, something struck the Audi from the side at speed. It created such a jolt that the big man's finger squeezed the trigger - blowing the driver's head apart. Blood, gore, and brain matter covered the windshield. Garrick caught a glimpse of the vehicle that had struck them. It was their hired BMW with Fanta at the wheel.

The impact on the slope twisted the Audi to the side. It was going so fast that it teetered for a second – then rolled over onto its side. Every loose item in the vehicle was lifted into the air as it rolled uncontrollably down the steep incline. Nobody was wearing a seat belt – so Tom and O'Connell were violently tossed around the cabin as windows shattered and broken glass added to the chaos. The driver's headless torso pinballed into them, splattering more blood like a fountain.

They struck something hard and came to an abrupt halt.

But Garrick no longer cared.

Chapter Twenty-Five

DCI David Garrick couldn't move. There was a throbbing in his head, and for several seconds, he was frightened that he was pinned in the back of the Audi. He opened his eyes... and a hospital ward swam into view.

The rhythmic sounds from monitors positioned just behind him assured him he was alive. Barely. A nurse peered at him with a smile.

"Don't try to move. You're fine."

But he wasn't fine, and he couldn't move. He was lying in a bed, unable to see the state of his own body. More nurses appeared, and a doctor who shone a light in Garrick's eyes. He appeared satisfied with whatever he was looking for.

"You'll be OK, David," the doctor assured him, then walked away.

Garrick tried to turn his head to call him back, but couldn't. Instead, he stopped paying attention to the ebb and flow of medics around him. He only had one burning question on his mind.

Siren's Call

An hour, maybe more, seemed to pass with his voice coming out as nothing more than a croak, and nobody offering him any news other than *he'll be fine*. Then, Fanta Liu appeared almost magically at his side. She was dressed in a black t-shirt, her shoulder-length hair combed straight as if she hadn't taken any time to look after it. Several red scratches covered her face, two of which were held together with stitches. Garrick guessed they were a consequence from ramming him off the road. But the most shocking thing was the tears rolling unchecked down her face.

"Guv..." She fought tears and tried to smile. "Looks like I lost my bet. You're alive."

He tried to say her name, but his mouth was dry. Fanta got the hint and poured water from a jug into a plastic cup.

"Hampstead Heath is a mess. O'Connell is alive. But he looks worse than you. They say he won't walk again. And he was impaled through the liver by a chunk of metal. Talk about irony. He'll need a new one."

She angled the cup so Garrick could sip the water.

"We recovered the laptop. It was a gold mine for the whole operation. Everybody he's paid off over here and in France. And the good news is, SCO19 were in charge of things. Not me. Although I suggested herding you into the park," she said with a trace of pride. "The Super hasn't fired me just yet–"

"Wendy..." Garrick finally gasped. He didn't care about the case.

Fanta's eyes grew wide. "Has nobody told you?"

Garrick tried to shake his head but couldn't.

Fanta looked around. "Maybe I should call a nurse..."

"Please," he gasped. "Wendy... the baby..."

"Do you know how long you've been unconscious?"

225

Garrick had an unexpected sense of feeling as Fanta took his hand and squeezed it. She licked her lips. Then she told him the news.

DIVE INTO BOOK 9 - A DEGREE OF MURDER - it's just a click away here!

A DEGREE OF MURDER
DCI GARRICK 9 - PRE-ODER NOW!

Also by M.G. COLE

BECOME A VIP
TAP TO JOIN THE FREE GROUP FOR EXCLUSIVES AND GET A FREE NOVELLA!

Twitter: @abriggswriter

Bluesky: @andybriggs42@bsky.social

SLAUGHTER OF INNOCENTS

DCI Garrick 1

MURDER IS SKIN DEEP

DCI Garrick 2

THE DEAD WILL TALK

DCI Garrick 3

DEAD MAN'S GAME

DCI Garrick 4

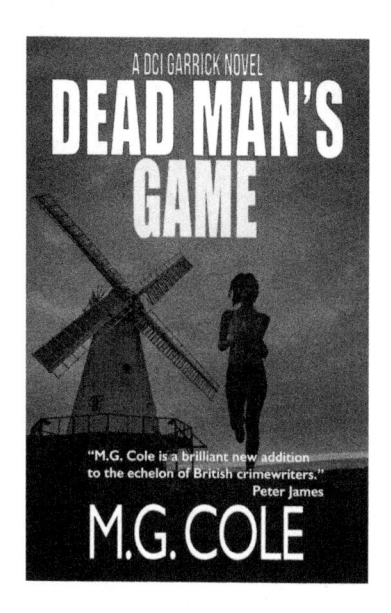

CLEANSING FIRES

DCI Garrick 5

THE DEAD DON'T PAY

DCI Garrick 6

A MURDER OF LIES

DCI Garrick 7

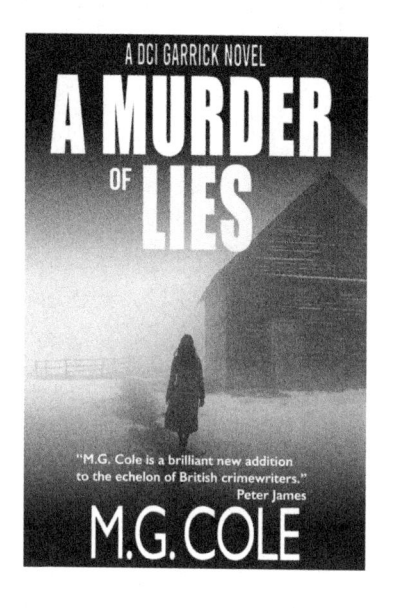

A DEGREE OF MURDER

DCI Garrick 9 - COMING SOON!

A DCI GARRICK NOVEL

A DEGREE OF MURDER

"M.G. Cole is a brilliant new addition to the echelon of British crimewriters."
Peter James

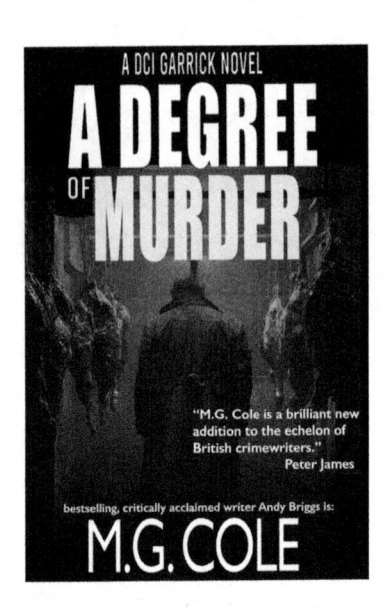

bestselling, critically acclaimed writer Andy Briggs is:

M.G. COLE